The Vampires of Atlantis

ATLANTIS
BOOK ONE

COURTNEY DAVIS

5 PRINCE PUBLISHING

Published by 5 PRINCE PUBLISHING & BOOKS, LLC

PO Box 865, Arvada, CO 80001

www.5PrinceBooks.com

ISBN digital: 978-1-63112-317-4

ISBN print: 978-1-63112-318-4

Cover Credit: Marianne Nowicki

06292023

To all the women I work with who keep reading what I write. A lot of this series was written on my lunch breaks so I think I should dedicate it to you all! Thanks for the encouragement. If you keep reading, I'll keep writing!

Acknowledgments

Thank you to the staff at 5 Prince Publishing for continuing to give me a chance with this whole author thing.

Thank you to the amazing Cate Byers who helps turn my story into the best it can be, I wouldn't have such a marketable product without you!

Other Titles by

COURTNEY DAVIS

The Serpent and the Firefly

A Spider in the Garden

Princess of Prias

The Vampires of Atlantis

The Vampires of Atlantis

One

≈

IAN HATED LEAVING THE WATER, his home and purpose in life, or death, depending on how you wanted to look at it. He was a vampire of Atlantis, a city sunken to contain monsters that had once threatened the lives of all on land. The horrible beasts that preyed on humans without thought or mercy. Vampires may have sipped from the humans, but it wasn't thoughtless, and it wasn't violent. The vampires were royalty, they were the chosen ones, they were the protectors, the warriors... and in return, they were given blood offerings. It was a small price for the humans to pay for their safety. The city was sunk into what was now called The Bermuda Triangle and for 12,000 years the vampires had done their job perfectly despite being betrayed and forgotten by the humans, and for the last five hundred years, Ian had been in charge. Nothing had gone wrong.

Until now.

Last night, Norgis had escaped. How the bastard had gotten out, Ian had no idea, but it was his responsibility to go above the waterline, find the monster, and return him.

It had probably been a thousand years since he'd set foot on land above the waterline, but he knew what to expect, they'd kept a close watch on the world above, updating their knowledge of customs and vocabulary for a scenario just like this. He resented the duty though. He would have preferred to send one of his trusted men, except this had never happened before. No monster had escaped in all these years, so he had to take care of it personally.

It wasn't even the monster-hunting that he begrudged. He actually looked forward to stretching his abilities once more and taking down the dumb beast. It was the possible run-in with the Aristotle Society that he wasn't looking forward to. The last time he'd been out of the water, he'd had a nasty encounter with them. Human bastards who thought they were special just because they were privy to the existence of Atlantis. They were more of a danger to humans with their little pets than vampires ever were. Ian hoped to avoid them this time.

His hand absently rubbed at a bite scar on his left arm. He wouldn't have time to stop and deal with them when there was a monster to contain.

The moon was high, and he took a moment to appreciate the sight of it. It should have been fully dark when he emerged, but garish, glaring lights were visible not far away and their brightness invaded the deserted beach. Ian stripped the wetness from his shoulder-length blond locks as he looked at his surroundings with disdain. From where he stood, he could see a few people moving about on the other side of the beach, could smell their warm blood. His fangs descended; it had been a while since a ship full of warm bodies had been taken to eat. During the last hundred years, he'd ordered the inhabitants of Atlantis to satiate themselves with large sea animals that hunters returned with. It was necessary in order to keep their secrets safe as human technology had advanced. Blood was blood, it did the job, but there was something special about taking it from the warm neck of a human. Ian supposed it reminded them of what it had been like when they were rewarded for their position of protection. When they'd accepted this life as guardians in the deep, it had been a thing of celebration, of offerings and bounty.

Ian brought his hunger under control and strode across the beach toward the light and noise. A group of young men stopped to stare from a nearby walkway.

"Yo, dude, what movie set did you just crawl out of?" one laughed.

"Yeah, you look like you belong on stage shaking your dick for cash!" another yelled and slapped his friend's back.

Ian grasped the sword that hung at his side and fisted his other hand. It was tempting to slit the throats of these idiots for thinking they could talk to him in such a manner. But he knew humans had forgotten him, forgotten what he was and how the vampires protected them from horrific death. He forced his body to calm. This wasn't a battle arena, and they weren't a threat, just dumb.

"What city is this?" he demanded.

"Miami, man. What's your deal? You fall off a cruise ship or something?" the first one called.

"Miami," Ian said slowly, testing the word on his tongue. He'd heard of this city. They tried to keep track of the changes above the waterline and this place, being so close to an entrance to Atlantis, had come up more than once. This is where the scent of Norgis had led him, and that meant it was no longer a safe place for humans. "Miami is in trouble, young men. I suggest you gather your weapons and protect your women." Ian strode forward. The scent of Norgis was faint and tainted. There were far too many strange smells up here distorting the trail, but he could still follow it.

"Where do you keep your ancient items of power?" Ian demanded. The group looked at him with blank stares, and Ian wondered if these were simpletons. "Where do you go to learn of your past and protect your future?" Ian prodded.

More blank stares.

"School?" one said without confidence.

Ian grunted and decided they were not going to be able to help him. He continued past, heading toward a wall of noise just beyond the trees.

"Dude's got a fucking sword!" one of the young men said as Ian strode past.

"Probably drunk," another said with a laugh.

The trees offered him cover and a moment to gather himself in shadows. He stood there hidden and watched, allowing himself to feel overwhelmed for a moment. The world was nothing like he remembered.

It was bright as day there beyond the trees and his green eyes, so used to the low lights of Atlantis, squinted against it as they tried to adjust. The sounds of so many people, music, and fast-moving vehicles assaulted his ears. He thought he must have made a mistake; he was not the one to do this. He should have sent someone else, someone who had more recently been above the waterline. This was not a world he knew anything about anymore. How could he keep himself hidden? How could he find Norgis? How could he do either of those things without killing every irritating blood-filled human that crossed his path?

Even as he thought it, a female dressed in tight fabric that barely covered her body approached and leaned against a tree, pushing her chest out to him. "Hey baby, is there something I can do for you? You look like Tarzan just crawled out of the ocean to play," she drawled.

Her breath was thick with sickness. No doubt her body was not long for this world. He didn't hold back his scowl at her, interrupting him. "You can offer me nothing, female. Go about your business and find a healer before it's too late."

"You are my business; I'll do you a handy for ten bucks, big fella." She reached for his sealskin leather kilt, but he batted her hand away easily.

His belt held his sword and a few other items he'd thought he might need, including gold coins. Ian pulled out one of the coins, realizing this female was a prostitute. He threw it at her feet and walked away.

"Idiots and whores," he said under his breath, "No wonder Norgis chose to come here. They will be easy to subjugate, even for him."

Ian moved along, following the hint of Norgis' stench, sticking mostly to shadows and watching the humans curiously. The men wore more clothing than he did, but many of the women wore less. Bits of cloth that only covered their sex and breasts. Could they all be whores? Perhaps he'd just come out into the part of town where the sexual tempters flourished at night. This would not be the place he would find Norgis who, he assumed, was after something magical to aid in whatever plan he'd managed to come up with. Or someone had come up with for him. Ian frowned as his mind circled around the idea that Norgis had been helped, had been released rather than escaped. Norgis was not the smartest monster in the prison, and Ian doubted he'd be able to come up with any plan on his own. That was a more worrying thought. If Norgis had help, that meant someone had betrayed Ian

The second time Ian was approached by a lone female offering her body for pay, he didn't smell sickness on her. Knowing he'd need the strength to concentrate on his task, he pulled her into his arms and to the shadow of a building. She moaned a practiced sound that he didn't for a moment believe, and he rolled his eyes as his fangs extended. He forced her head to the side, exposing her soft neck. He could smell her blood pumping steadily just under the surface. She wasn't afraid, but she should be. His head dipped; anticipation high as he thought of taking the sweet blood of a warm human into his mouth once again.

He froze millimeters from piercing her flesh.

A scent drifted to him and stilled his body. Every one of his cells rippled with a strange electricity. He dropped the female he'd been holding and a gold coin for her trouble, ignoring her grunts of outrage.

Unable to ignore the scent, he stalked through a dark alley and across a street, hiding in shadow, his eyes sought out the one whose blood had awakened something deep within him, had lit a fire that even now was burning through him with an intensity he'd never experienced. He didn't at first understand, but when his eyes landed on her, his heart stopped, and he knew. His instincts raged at him to move, to grab her and run. To claim her before anyone else could. The only thing stopping him, she wasn't alone, and he knew enough of this modern world to hesitate, to watch and wait. Females didn't take kindly to being stolen away.

He studied her from a distance, drinking in every inch of her he could see. Hair as black as night that reached almost to her waist and a slight body wrapped tightly in a white dress that showed a lot of long, tan leg and bare arms. He ached to touch that skin, to smell it and taste it. He envied everyone who was closer to her, everyone that was able to see or smell her better than he could.

When she turned, her eyes scanning curiously into the darkness where he'd slunk, he could tell they were eyes as blue as the ocean in her perfectly round face with pink lips and sharp eyebrows. He wanted her to see him, wanted to watch recognition form in her eyes, recognition that he was the last male she'd ever need or want. He was destined to have her as his own and she had to be feeling it, too.

Katherine hated dates. Group or not, this was torture. Her favorite coworker, Jenny, had begged her to double date. Her boyfriend Max's cousin was in town and wanted to see the Miami nightlife. Katherine had only agreed because Jenny was such a good friend, and even more so because she had laughed at a joke when she didn't know Katherine could hear, about the cobwebs that must be between Katherine's legs.

Katherine knew she needed to get back out in the dating

THE VAMPIRES OF ATLANTIS

world. Her near marriage had ended over two years ago, but she just wasn't interested in dating another idiot who would take her money and her dog and leave her with nonrefundable wedding deposits. She knew that was a very specific scenario that would probably not occur again, especially since she didn't currently own a dog, but still, why risk it? She had a good job at the museum, she liked to read, and she liked to be alone. It was a safe life, maybe a little boring, but safe.

Jenny was fun, and it showed in her short black hair and spunky style. She was filled with a joy for life and an energy she must have been born with. Her good mood always rubbed off on Katherine, which is one reason she'd gravitated toward Jenny for friendship. Katherine knew she needed someone to lift her up out of her dumped funk and Jenny had been that person for the last six months. Tonight was the first time she'd actually let Jenny convince her to get out on a sort of date, though. Katherine had to admit it was probably time, but tonight's company wasn't exactly her type.

So here she was with Jenny and Max, and the blind date, Tony, at a crowded bar near the beach. It wasn't terrible, as far as a night out went. Tony was nice and didn't try to make it feel too much like a date. He was from out of town and dressed like a tourist in tan cargo shorts and a flamboyant shirt. She never would have picked him for a date if she'd seen him in the bar or club. He seemed to sense her hesitation and only got close when it looked like another guy was going to approach. She appreciated that.

They were standing outside the club, debating on hitting another or calling it a night, when she felt a strange sensation, a feeling of being watched. There were people everywhere, of course, and she darted her gaze around, not noticing anyone in particular looking her way.

She shivered as the feeling intensified, a chill running through her despite the warm Florida night.

"Are you cold?" Tony asked, reaching out and rubbing her arms briskly.

A sound reached her ears then, something unrecognizable, something animalistic. She turned her head again, eyes scanning for danger. She saw nothing, but expected to be attacked by a panther at any second.

"Oh no, are you ill?" Jenny asked with concern. "Oh my god, did you get roofied?"

A look of horror passed over Tony's face at the suggestion. He was a nice guy.

"No, I don't think so. I just think I might be coming down with something. Perhaps I should call it a night." It was a perfect excuse to end this evening of pretend dating. "I'll just grab a cab; you guys go on to the next club and have fun."

"Are you sure? I could see that you get home safe?" Tony offered gallantly.

"Uh, no, thanks though. I really don't feel well and I don't want to ruin everyone's night." She gave him a weak smile of apology. "My stomach is bad, probably from the clams in there. I'll see you tomorrow, Jenny. Hope you have a great rest of your vacation, Tony."

Katherine held out a hand for a cab.

"If you're sure you're okay to get home," Jenny said with a sigh, not at all believing that Katherine was sick.

"I'm fine," Katherine assured her. "I'm a big girl."

"You're five feet tall and a hundred pounds. You could get taken out by a strong wind," Jenny laughed and gave Katherine a tight hug. "Thanks for coming out," she whispered in her ear. "You lasted longer than I expected."

"Rude," Katherine laughed, pulling away. "See you tomorrow."

A cab had stopped, and Katherine hopped in, breathing a sigh of relief after she gave her address and it pulled away from the curb.

"Bad date?" the driver asked with a quick glance over his shoulder.

"It wasn't really a date, but aren't they all bad?" she said with a laugh.

"Only if you've given up on love."

Katherine gave the back of the man's head a frown. He had grey hair and wrinkled skin, he was wearing a button-up shirt and the cab smelled surprisingly clean. If she had to guess, he was a retired grandpa doing this to keep himself busy. Maybe his wife had died, and he just had to get out, get some social interaction. He'd found love in a time when people married at eighteen and didn't divorce, no matter what. Nowadays, with divorce almost a certainty, her broken engagement was probably a blessing. It could have been worse. Kids could have been involved.

But had she given up on love? She didn't feel very hopeful of it, that's for sure. Healthy skepticism is what she'd been telling herself, but maybe it was something more. Maybe something had broken when Steve had left her. She suddenly felt very alone and couldn't wait to sit down with one of her fantasy romance novels. Spending time with fictional men with superhuman abilities who couldn't hurt her, like Steve had, seemed like a much better use of her time.

Two

IAN HAD A CHOICE TO MAKE, follow the one who made his blood run hot, or destroy the one who had dared to touch her. Never in his life had he wanted to expend so much energy destroying a stranger than he had in the moments he watched the male touch her arms with familiarity and comfort. The only thing that had saved the man was that the interaction had ended quickly, and she'd then left the group in a yellow vehicle. She was getting away fast, so he'd left the stranger to kill another time and followed her as best he could on foot, her trailing scent tantalizing him. He ignored the questioning looks from those he passed and all the strange sights of the unfamiliar city. All that mattered was her. She was calling to his soul, and he intended to answer.

He didn't expect that he'd run across the strong scent of Norgis, derailing him momentarily from his path. The scent was fresh enough that he couldn't ignore it, and he followed it to a building that also held the lingering scent of her. She'd been here, recently and often, though he could tell that neither she nor Norgis were still inside. The mix of her scent with Norgis' sent a spike of fear and anger through him that was unexpected in its intensity. To know she could ever be in danger from that monster had him gripping his sword and wanting to take her to Atlantis and lock her in a room where she would always be safe, and with him.

The building in front of him was large with many windows and proclaimed Museum. It didn't surprise him at all that Norgis had sought it out. Even Ian could tell the building held artifacts as ancient as Norgis himself. Their scent and the pull of past magics prickled across his skin from where he stood outside. What might Norgis have gained at a place such as this? And how was his female involved?

She was his, no question in his mind about it.

He knew Norgis wasn't in the building still. He could come back to investigate it later. He continued on the fresh scent of his female. She was his new top priority, especially if she was mixed in with whatever Norgis was after. Ian soon came to a tall building that smelled as if it housed many people. This must be where she lived. He pulled on a glass door. It was locked. He peered in at a large room with sparse furnishings and many other doors along all sides. He knew he could easily break in if necessary. No pane of glass or steel was going to keep him from her, but he hesitated. He didn't want to approach her in a frightening manner if he could help it, couldn't bear the thought of seeing fear in her eyes as she looked upon him.

He retreated to shadow and waited, debating his next move. He knew what he should be doing, what was expected of him, but he never could have predicted this beautiful complication. Now nothing mattered to him more than the female that was calling to him. Once she was safely his, then he could focus on Norgis.

❧

Katherine lived in a small apartment on the third floor of a building near enough to the museum where she worked that she was able to walk. She had as much space as she needed here and she was never happier than when she was on her couch in stretchy pants and a baggy shirt, reading or watching old movies. Ten minutes after getting into her apartment, that's exactly what she was doing. A little too energized to sleep just yet, despite the late hour, she settled in with a glass of wine and started going through the channels, looking for something that would settle her mind and allow her to sleep. Or maybe a good rom com that would make her cry and laugh and fall asleep with the dream that her very own sexy and unexpected love interest was perhaps waiting just around the corner. She took a big sip of her wine and decided she didn't need to settle for less than epic level romance. Maybe she was lonely at times, maybe she was finally ready to move on from her heartbreak, but that didn't mean she was interested in just anyone. She wanted to be swept off her feet, tossed in the air and embraced by someone who knocked her socks off with a look.

It wasn't too much to ask for, was it?

She flipped through the channels and stopped when she came to a documentary about a dig in South America that was unearthing some history-changing artifacts from the Inca. She settled in to watch, fascinated by the history and adventure. If she'd never met Steve, then she never would have turned down the study abroad program. But she hadn't wanted to ruin their new relationship. She could have gone to Egypt and worked with archeologists for real world experience, and then she might have become the one bringing new things to light in Ecuador. Instead, she'd let her life take a safer route. She was good at her job at the museum, but it wasn't what she'd dreamed of when she was young.

A harsh knock on the door jarred her out of her disappointing memories. She spilled her wine and dropped the remote, staring at the offending door. Another knock, and a yell this time.

"Katherine, are you in there? Answer your goddamn door. I've been calling you!" It was Richard, her boss at the museum.

Katherine grunted in annoyance but got up and answered the door, anyway. "Come on in, Richard," she hissed, flinging the door open, then going to the kitchen for a rag. "You scared the shit out of me. I spilled my wine."

"Sorry, but seriously what, you don't answer your phone anymore?"

"I was out."

The look of shock on his face was a healthy reminder that she needed to get out more. "Oh... I just assumed you were home."

"Yeah, well I am now."

"Alone?" he questioned with a quick glance around.

"Yes, alone," she snapped. "What couldn't wait until tomorrow?"

"Someone broke into the museum."

That got her attention. She froze mid cleanup and stared at Richard, hoping he was joking. "What?"

"I need you to get down there. You're the only one who can tell what's missing. They tore through the public displays and the storage. It's a mess."

"Shit."

"Yeah, so get cleaned up and let's go," Richard said, pushing his glasses up his nose. He was a typical middle-aged man; losing his red hair, gaining a pot belly, and dressed like he taught math or something equally boring. He had an ex-wife, three children he saw on weekends, and Katherine knew that he kept a bottle of vodka in his desk. But he took his job at the museum seriously and he knew a lot about the museum's artifacts and history in general. She respected him and felt a bit sorry for him.

"I'll be ready in two minutes." Katherine hurried to her bedroom and pulled on a pair of jeans and a clean t-shirt, slipped her feet into running shoes and pulled her long black hair back into a ponytail. It probably took less than five minutes before she was locking the door behind them. "Did you call the police already?"

"Yeah, but until we know what was taken, it's hardly more serious than breaking and entering with destruction of property.

No witnesses and the cameras blanked out, I already checked, so we probably won't be able to find the idiots unless they try to pawn something or sell it online."

"Kids just trying to make a mess?" Katherine reasoned.

"Could be, but it seems rather targeted to the exhibits on island life of the Caribbean and the recent shipment in from the shipwreck."

They left her building and started off at a fast pace to the museum. Katherine felt a prickle at the back of her neck again, like she was being watched. A tingle in her spine like she'd had outside the bar. Her mind stayed focused on the problem at work, distracting her from whatever her body was trying to tell her, and she didn't even bother looking around. She would have seen a half-naked stranger with a sword at his side watching her from the shadows, barely holding himself back from attacking the man she walked with.

When Katherine and Richard got to the museum, she nearly broke down in tears. She'd been working there for ten years, had organized, labeled, boxed, and carefully stored thousands of artifacts in the storage. She had set up beautiful artifacts in displays on the museum floor for others to enjoy and learn from. So much of her recent work was destroyed in one night of pointless vandalism. At least it seemed pointless to her. If someone had been looking for something here, why would they break so much to search for it?

"It's going to take weeks to figure this out," she whispered. "There's no way to tell if anything is missing. There is certainly a lot of priceless irreplaceable artifacts destroyed, I can see that right off," she told the policeman who was trying to get a statement.

"Can you estimate the value of the damage, Ma'am?"

Katherine slow turned and blinked up at the officer. All five feet of her was boiling with anger, barely holding back a snarky comment, she gritted out, "Priceless, irreplaceable artifacts from thousands of years ago!"

"Right, okay. I'll just put down that you'll have an estimate of damage after further investigation."

"You do that," she hissed, not in any mood to deal with this idiot. She wanted to start looking through the piles and figuring out what was salvageable. She glanced around and reassessed the damage. This was going to take months.

Richard came over then and the officer was thankful to turn from her and ask him questions instead. No doubt she was close to being called a hostile witness, but she didn't care. Tears stung her eyes as she bent down and lifted a piece of broken pottery that had survived from the height of the Roman era, now gone at the hands of some teenage idiots trying to have a good time at someone else's expense. Never in her life had she felt such rage, such a desire to kill another person. Not even Steve's betrayal had cut this deep.

If she'd wanted to investigate that, she'd probably have to realize he'd been right when he accused her of loving her job more than him. But there was no way she was willing to admit that asshole had been right about any damn thing.

Katherine settled in to do the heartbreaking work, to pick through the damage for anything salvageable. To label, box, and store things that would never be good enough to display again. Their stories of history no longer readable.

"Kids suck," she grumbled.

"Yeah, they do," an officer agreed from nearby. "Probably a high school prank, a dare maybe. Why they had to take it so far is beyond me, and how the hell they managed to knock out the cameras and security system? It's like they set off an EMP that only affected this building."

"An electromagnetic pulse," another officer scoffed. "Right, like any of the high schools around here are teaching kids at that level. This was professionals."

Katherine frowned and looked around at the mess. An electromagnetic pulse? She'd heard of those from her neighbor, Larry, who she was pretty sure wore a lot of tinfoil hats and hadn't left the apartment building in years. He was always warning her that some other country was going to take out all the electronics with an EMP bomb and nothing would work anymore. Then we'd be invaded, of course, enslaved maybe. He told her at least once a month that it was probably happening soon and, when it did, he would happily take her with him to his hideout in the woods. She thanked him politely because the last thing she wanted to do was piss off the crazy man in her building, but she was pretty sure she'd rather take her chances with an invading army than with him alone in a cabin. EMPs were definitely not high school level prank technology. Could this have been done by some crazy collector, some rich tech wizard who's really into pottery dragged up from the bottom of the ocean? Seemed like a stretch. She pulled out her cell to tell Jenny what was going on, but the screen was blank.

Three

~~~

IAN STOOD in shadow outside the museum where there were too many people for him to risk getting close. He couldn't tell what was happening inside, but he watched and waited. Did this have to do with Norgis? What had he done in there and why was she here now? Had something been taken? Had Norgis found something that he could use to further whatever plan he had? Norgis with a plan, that didn't feel right. Ian worried, not for the first time, that Norgis had help, that he was working as someone else's dumb muscle. That would make him harder to track and take down. Of all the monsters housed in the bowels of Atlantis, Norgis had one of the simplest minds. Easy to control and powerful, but to come up with this on his own was unlikely. Had one of his men helped the monster escape?

Ian had so many questions and it irked him to not be in the know. It was a new experience for him.

The only comfort was that she would not leave without him knowing. It was many hours until sunrise and he doubted she would stay that long; humans were not nocturnal creatures. And when she returned home, he wouldn't let a locked door keep him from her, that he vowed.

What little he could pick up on conversations had him wondering about their lack of usable electric devices. Had Norgis affected them somehow? There was no telling how a beast as ancient as Norgis might affect a modern world. Had whoever Norgis was working with done something to the building to cover their tracks from humans? The humans seemed confused and concerned as well, which told him it must be something beyond their capability and understanding.

Ian studied the people coming and going. Many were dressed alike in a uniform of some kind and held weapons. They must be the law keepers. Others were dressed similar to the female had been when she'd left her home. Blue thick pants and shirts. Ian looked down at his own attire and frowned. If he was going to try to fit in, he would have to think about changing his clothes. He was very good at hiding, however, and as long as he stayed in shadows unmoving, he knew it was difficult for human eyes to see him.

"My king, it's been a long time," a voice said behind him, making him turn and draw his sword.

"Beltar," Ian said quietly, lowering his sword but not putting it away. "I'm not your king. I haven't taken up my father's crown."

Beltar shrugged, "Details."

The vampire was standing near, and it was disconcerting that Ian hadn't heard him approach. He'd been too distracted watching for the female. Beltar was dressed like the humans except his pants were black and he wore a shirt with buttons. He had cut his blond hair very short, but left it spiked up the middle of his head in a fearsome style. There was a sword hanging from his back. Ian could see its handle above Beltar's right shoulder, easily accessible, and Ian knew from experience that Beltar could have it out and in the neck of an enemy in a blink. He was a true warrior and a friend.

"I can only assume you are here because of Norgis?" Beltar added when Ian didn't respond.

"Yes, he escaped, and I tracked him here."

"I came across his scent this evening as well and followed it here. It's been a long time since I've seen you above the waterline. I would have expected you'd send Thorn, or perhaps Saul."

"I'm in charge. If someone managed to escape, it's my responsibility to take care of it," Ian said bitterly, the sting of failure still new.

"Norgis is no longer in there," Beltar pointed out.

"No," Ian agreed, unwilling to admit he was here to catch a female.

Beltar raised an eyebrow, his blue eyes assessing. "And yet you wait."

Ian looked back at the building with yearning, then at his old friend. "I was hoping to discover what Norgis might have gained here. The humans haven't decided if anything is missing."

"Humans are idiots, they may never figure it out. Come, let's hunt monsters together."

Ian had little choice but to agree. He didn't want to bring the female to the attention of Beltar. He knew where she lived and where she spent her days. He would not lose her if he left now. Of course, that didn't settle his anger as he turned from the building where she was. He couldn't keep her safe if he wasn't near. "Yes, let's hunt," Ian hissed. He would take his anger and frustration out on Norgis.

They tracked the damn thing through the city and into the sewers below but lost it and had to call it a loss, as the sun was threatening to come up.

"I am honored to have you in my coven house for the day's rest," Beltar said, showing Ian through an old barn, down a trap door and staircase, into a bunker hollowed out of the earth beneath.

It was a nice setup, really. The walls were stone, but the floor had been covered in wood planks, making for a warm feeling. Electricity was hooked up, allowing for lights and other conveniences. Beltar was leader of a coven of five vampires who had left Atlantis, choosing to serve as a go-between of the above the waterline and below, keeping the Atlantean vampires apprised of world events and trends to a certain extent. This was to ensure that any of them could come above and not be completely overwhelmed by the changes. Beltar's coven consisted of himself, Samson, Laric, Trenton, and Prat, all warriors, all vampires, and all to be feared. Not by Ian, who had been with them centuries ago as they grew into their warrior statuses, but by any enemy who crossed their paths. Ian had planned to seek them out immediately after arriving on land and gain their assistance with this search for Norgis. Of course, he'd been distracted and thrown off track by the female.

"No way! Ian is here!" Laric yelled as they came into the main room of the underground home. "I haven't seen you since I fled that underwater tomb!"

"Laric, my old friend, it isn't that bad down there," Ian exclaimed, clapping his friend on the back as they embraced.

Laric wore his long blond hair loose about his body and his blue eyes were wide with happiness at seeing his friend. "Not so bad, huh. Then why are you up here with us?"

"Norgis," Samson growled, coming into the room. "I scented the damn monster near the water earlier, lost him. Glad you're here, Ian. Someone with half a brain needs to be in charge." The hostility he threw at Beltar with his narrowed purple eyes worried Ian, but he wasn't here to rearrange their lives and pecking order. Samson couldn't make it down below because he had a problem with authority. Apparently that hadn't changed.

Samson ran a hand through his short black hair as he stalked to the edge of the room and laid down his weapons. He was a huge man, as large as Ian and by far the biggest of the coven here. He looked like a warrior from the past and Ian wondered how well he was doing blending in. Perhaps he'd have to talk to Beltar about moving the man back down to Atlantis. If he was going to be unhappy anyway, he might as well be where he wouldn't alert humans.

"I'm sure we will find him tomorrow night," Beltar said placatingly. "Then Ian can return to ruling his underwater empire."

"In such a rush to leave?" Prat asked as he and Trenton came in. They looked half drunk and must have been feeding. Judging by the scent of blood and sex on them, they were doing more than just taking blood. They were the youngest of the group, twins who had wild streaks and had come above the waterline seeking adventure. They still had young faces and wide smiles, with a youthfulness that in reality was long gone. Brown eyes and hair on both of them. The only difference between the two was Trenton kept his hair short and Prat's was long and pulled back into a ponytail that hit his shoulders. Ian had never enjoyed the company of the brothers, too excitable, too unpredictable. He hoped Beltar had a better handle on them than it appeared.

Ian gave Beltar a questioning look and got a shrug in return.

"I do hope you spend a little time. There are some delightful things above the waterline," Trenton agreed heartily.

"I can see you've enjoyed yourselves tonight," Beltar said carefully. "Did you not smell the stench of Norgis in our territory?"

"Yeah, of course," they hastily agreed. "But we also smelled Ian, so we knew it was getting taken care of. No use in all of us chasing the same monster."

"Indeed," Beltar hissed. "Ian, I am sure you'll be comfortable back here for the day's rest. When the sun goes down, I can show you the best place to find an easy meal."

"That shouldn't be necessary," Ian said. "I ate recently and feel no need to now." What he didn't say was that he very much wanted to feed but would settle for nothing less than the sweetest being he'd ever scented and would be seeking her out as soon as the sun went down. The longer he went without satisfying the need for her, the deeper it burned.

Samson eyed him suspiciously but didn't say anything.

"Is it just the one successful prison break?" Laric asked.

"He's the only monster that got out and none of my men are missing," Ian said.

"Then how the hell did the thing get out?" Samson demanded.

"That's what I intend to find out," Ian said with deadly calm.

Samson gave an approving nod, and the twins hooted as if they were about to embark on a wild hunt right that moment.

"We will all be helping with that," Beltar assured him.

Ian had to hold himself back from denying the need for help. "It should be over quickly, then."

"And you can return to Atlantis," Samson said.

But not alone, he told himself.

Beltar showed Ian to a small room with a bed, washbasin, and dresser. It wasn't much, but it was enough. "You can borrow some clothes tomorrow if you want to blend a little better."

"I appreciate the hospitality, Beltar."

"As if I could do anything less for the Prince of Atlantis," Beltar laughed and shut the door. Ian stretched out on the bed and stared up at the rock ceiling as images of the female filled his mind. He swore he could still smell her. He closed his eyes and inhaled deeply, but he only caught whiffs of the other vampires and their recent prey. Nothing as sweet and enticing as his female. More than anything, he wished he knew her name.

Katherine got home an hour before sunrise and fell into bed exhausted, woke up a couple hours later and was back at it. She was working her way through the mess, painfully slowly. Cataloging each item, checking off broken, or not and repairable or not. So far, she had no idea if anything was missing, didn't think she would know for sure for at least a few weeks, maybe longer, if ever. Whoever had done this had left behind destruction, almost as if that had been their only goal. The police had no leads, millions of fingerprints; it was a museum. *Don't touch* signs screamed touch me, and people had, all over the damn place. Whoever had done this was most likely going to get away with it unless she figured out that they took something, and then they tried to sell it somewhere, which made Katherine even more determined to get through the piles and figure out if even one tiny stone was missing. Assuming it wasn't an international art thief who would be selling the item on the black market... spy perhaps? They still weren't able to get power in the building beyond the lights. It was as if whatever the criminals had done, it only affected wifi and bluetooth. Interrupting cameras, computers, and cellphones. Far too advanced for someone who was going to run to a pawn shop, which meant they were not likely to be able to track them down even if she did figure out what was missing.

"Fuck," she hissed as the futility of her efforts invaded her mind.

"Katherine, did you stop to eat today?" Jenny asked, picking her way through the mess at about five in the afternoon.

"Umm... I'm not sure, to be honest." Katherine said with a sigh, setting down her notebook. "I think I had some coffee."

"Yeah, that's what I thought. Let's go. You have to eat, or you will die. It's the human condition," Jenny said with a laugh.

"Okay, but we'll make it quick." Katherine stood up and stretched, she didn't want to stop, but knew that if she took a break and ate, she'd last longer into the night, and she didn't plan to stop until she couldn't keep her eyes open any longer.

"So, did you have fun last night?" Jenny asked as they sat down with their taco truck meals.

It was the closest decent food and once Katherine had decided to eat, she realized she was famished.

"Yeah, it was fine," Katherine said noncommittally.

"So... you'd want to do it again? Tony really liked you; he was super worried that you had food poisoning or got roofied or something."

Katherine took a big bite so she didn't have to answer right away. She had no interest in Tony, but she was pretty sure Jenny knew that. What Jenny was really asking was; *Are you finally over your heartbroken solitude and ready to get out there?* Katherine swallowed dramatically. She was over the broken heart, yes, and she was ready to try again, but she was going to hold out for the whole swept off her feet thing, nothing less.

"You know it's not good to be alone. We weren't built that way. We need companionship," Jenny continued.

"I want to be overwhelmed. I want all-consuming passion and all that," she sighed dramatically. "Maybe I'll just get a cat."

"You need a dick," Jenny said matter-of-factly, making Katherine choke on her soda. "Something to take the edge off. Fuck consuming passion, just get out there."

"I have one. It's ribbed and came with batteries."

It was Jenny's turn to choke, and she laughed so hard she drew the attention of everyone around them. "Katherine, you are too funny and too cute to be alone!"

"I appreciate the confidence boost, but I don't want to settle for an alright date. I don't know, maybe I'm crazy, but I want to be swept off my feet this time. I want him to work for it so hard he would never even consider leaving me. I want it to be real and forever."

Jenny sighed dramatically. "You might read too many romance novels, but I can't tell you that you're wrong. Romance and passion, it's a must."

"And no offense to Tony, he seemed like a sweet guy, but he didn't strike me as the type who sweeps girls off their feet."

"Definitely not. He's an optometrist from Kansas. I doubt he even knows what passion is. Honestly, I think you scared him a little. you were far too capable."

"A hazard of being alone. I do everything for myself."

"Hence the battery-operated dick," Jenny said, holding her paper cup up to cheers.

Katherine obliged, and they both fell into a fit of laughter.

"I was thinking about something new, actually," Katherine admitted.

"Oh, like you are going to try women?" Jenny asked, without judgment.

Katherine smiled, "No, actually I was thinking about trying to get on with a dig team. Go do some real hands-on work in the field while I'm still young and unattached."

"That would be great for you! Didn't you say you almost went once?"

"Yeah, before I met Steve. I might look into it. I need to do something to shake up my life before I wake up one day and realize it all passed me by and all I did was catalogue other people's discoveries."

"You're more adventurous than me. I couldn't handle all that dirt and those creepy crawlies in caves too. No, thank you," Jenny said with a shudder.

"I'll find it and you'll display it. How about that?" Katherine asked.

"Great plan. We'll be an amazing team."

Katherine sighed as she finished her meal. She really did think it was time to make a big change, and she wasn't getting any younger. If she could get on with a dig team, she'd be starting at the bottom with people in their early twenties. She'd have to prove herself among them, but she had a lot of knowledge to back her up. She could do it, and she had nothing holding her in Miami.

After they'd eaten, they walked back to the museum. Everyone had gone home, it seemed, and Jenny hugged Katherine goodbye at the back door. Katherine let herself in and went in search of her abandoned notebook next to the pile she'd been going through. She found it and settled back in.

The silence around her was deep, but that didn't bother her. She was used to quiet. She soon slipped into the zone, picking up items and assessing them one after another. She paused to stare longer at the item in her hand, confused and thrilled, it had her full attention until something prickled her skin and turned her stomach sour. A smell was the first thing she could put her finger on, it was unlike anything she'd ever smelled before. Thick and wet, it was like seaweed that had rotted in a vat of dead fish. About the time her mind was milling over the possibility that the smell was coming from a broken artifact, she heard a noise, like a scraping, a rustling, and every cell in her body screamed, *run!*

Four

IAN NEARLY LOST it when he smelled her blood. He knew right away he wasn't just smelling her; he was smelling her blood spilled, and a lot of it. Rage covered his fear, and he flew across the parking lot as fast as he could, thankful he'd not worn the silly pants that Beltar had offered him. He had taken a t-shirt, however, so he would blend a bit better and a pair of shoes that Laric had as extra. Sword drawn, he stopped at the door and listened. He could hear nothing inside, and his heart sank. If she was dead, he wasn't sure what he would do. He could smell Norgis strongly as well. He was here, or had been very recently. No doubt he was to blame for the spilled blood. The woman—Samson had informed him that calling them *female* tended to be offensive—had been harmed by the monster that he never should have let escape. This was all his fault.

Guilt tightened his gut as he eased the door open just enough to slip inside. The smell of Norgis mixed with the woman's blood was even stronger, and it was difficult for him to keep his head, to not rage and scream and run into the unknown seeking revenge. He was a practiced warrior; he knew better than to go into a fight with emotion rather than thought.

The building was dark and eerily quiet. The sound of him shutting the door reverberated through the room and if anyone was lying in wait, there would be no surprising them. Still, Ian waited, searched with his eyes, ears, and nose for danger, and for her.

When he identified a lump on the ground that was most definitely bloodier than the other splotches around, he lost his intent to be stealthy. He ran to it and knelt beside the tiny form. "Oh gods! What has happened to you?" He touched her gently, rolling her onto her back. There was a large gash on her throat and arm, as if she'd raised it to defend herself. Her eyes were closed, her face pale, and blood was everywhere. She'd been wearing a white shirt and it was almost solid red now. Ian pressed his head to her chest, listening for a heartbeat. So close to her, with so much blood, his fangs descended and ached to be fed, but he ignored them. The only thing that mattered was her. Was she alive?

Faintly, so very faintly, he could hear her heart and his entire body switched modes. She was alive, he had to help her. He did a quick search of her body and found no other open wounds. It looked like she had a broken leg though and a bruise was beginning to show on her cheek that indicated she'd taken quite a hit there, either from her attacker or the ground. He couldn't be sure, and it didn't matter. She was alive, but barely. Her wounds were great, and it was all his fault. He would do anything to save her, though, and he would tear Norgis apart with his bare hands for this.

Ian was beyond thankful that he'd found her first. He didn't trust humans to know how to keep her alive at this point and even if they could, it wouldn't be nearly as fast as what he could do for her. She was so far gone; he could feel how weak her heart was. A human might give up on her at this point, but he knew better. As long as the heart was beating, there was a chance to heal. He ripped into his own arm with his fangs and pressed the gushing wound to her lips as he held her head gently.

"Drink, dear one, drink and heal. I cannot live without you; I know I cannot." His words were fierce, and he watched with growing horror as she laid there unmoving, not reacting. "Why isn't it working?" he hissed.

"What did you do, Ian?"

The voice was jarring in the silence. Ian spun around and grabbed the woman in his arms, protecting her from the danger. His whole body was primed and ready to strike, to kill any who would dare harm her. When his mind registered that his eyes were seeing Samson standing halfway between him and the door, he didn't relax. "Get out of here, you cannot be here, there is too much blood!"

"Yeah, I smelled it a block away. I thought perhaps you had killed Norgis, but it seems you've killed something else," he said carefully. "You know, we aren't supposed to be killing humans up here." His voice was low and steady, but there was an edge to it, an accusation.

"I didn't kill her," Ian hissed. "Norgis tried to, and I am trying to heal her, but I don't know why it isn't working." There was a crackle to his voice that revealed his fright at the situation, but he didn't care if Samson sensed weakness in him at this moment. All that mattered was her.

Samson narrowed his eyes at Ian and flared his nostrils. "Smells warm enough. She isn't dead."

"I know! She won't take my blood, though." Ian was feeling frantic, shoving his arm against her mouth, forcing her lips to part but she still wasn't swallowing. Was it because of the neck wound?

"May I approach?" Samson asked carefully.

Ian realized he had drawn his sword and still held it out toward his comrade. He lowered it but didn't sheath it. "Do you know something I do not?"

"I've been up here a long while. I know a bit about humans, yes." Samson walked over carefully and knelt down. "Things you have perhaps forgotten."

Ian reluctantly loosened his grip so that Samson could examine her.

Samson sucked in a sharp breath and Ian hissed.

"She's quite something under all that blood, isn't she?" Samson whispered.

"Fuck you, fix her!" Ian was going to lose his mind, he was certain. Samson was the last person he would trust with a woman if he had any other option.

Samson grunted. "She's too far gone to swallow on her own and with that large neck wound, I can't massage her throat to force some of the blood into her stomach. I think you will have to drip it directly into the neck, then we can bind it. It *might* work."

"It has to work," Ian said, ripping into his arm again. The wound gushed fresh, and he pressed it against her neck wound while Samson watched doubtfully.

"Norgis did this?" Samson asked.

"I believe so. It smells like he came back. There's something here he wants; or wanted. She's key to figuring out what that might be," Ian said, hoping that Samson would believe that was why he was so concerned about this human's survival.

Samson's raised eyebrow told him he'd failed.

After a few agonizing minutes, her breathing changed slightly, and the sound of her heartbeat strengthened. Samson looked surprised as he offered his shirt to wrap the wound. "If I wrap it tight and the healing has started, she may be able to take more through her mouth now."

Ian moved his arm off of her neck and to her mouth as Samson carefully wrapped the wound. It wasn't pulsing out blood any longer, but it still looked deep. He wanted to lash out at his friend to tell him to be gentle, but he stopped himself, concentrating on the feel of her lips against his skin, they were too cold and unmoving. As Samson sat back on his heels, the makeshift bandage in place on her neck, Ian felt the muscles of her chin flex where he held her mouth open. He let go of her chin and her lips moved against his arm, drinking in the healing nectar that was his blood.

The thrill that went through him was unexpected. His whole body shivered, and a gasp escaped his lips. She was suckling at his arm, drawing the blood from his body of her own volition. It was the most intimate and erotic thing that had ever happened to him, and sharing the moment with Samson was horribly disconcerting. He was thankful for her body being across his lap to hide his erection.

Samson's face was somehow stone cold and angry at the same time as he witnessed the intimate moment. Ian wondered what could possibly be going through the man's mind, but he had a feeling he didn't want to know.

"She's had enough unless you plan to turn her," Samson finally said.

It was difficult for Ian to pull his arm from her, but he did. He had no intention of turning an unsuspecting human into a vampire, that never went well, and females rarely survived the change. "Her heartbeat is strong, but her body is still badly broken," Ian pointed out.

"It will take time. I would bet she'll sleep for a day or more while the blood works on her wounds. She was as close to dead as one can get and still be brought back with the blood, I think."

"I'll take her back to the bunker. She'll be safe there," Ian said, even as he wished there was a private place he could take her, away from the others. He momentarily considered her home, but that would never work. Even if he managed to find her rooms among the many and remain unseen, it would not be light tight.

"She's covered in blood, still bleeding a little, she's broken and near death... you are going to bring her underground with five other vampires?" Samson's tone clearly stated what an idiot he thought Ian was for even considering such a thing.

"I can't exactly leave her to heal on her own!" Ian hissed. "And

I can't let her go to a human healer, they'd notice something off about the quickness of her recovery."

Samson narrowed his eyes and grunted, not buying the excuse. "What is she to you?" He took a deep breath and his eyes widened slightly, but he didn't say anything.

Ian wasn't sure what Samson was noticing, but he didn't like that Samson was taking an interest. She couldn't be anything to Samson, because she was everything to him. He looked down at the small, bloody, and broken body with the beautiful face. She was inexplicably his new reason for breathing. "She has information about Norgis. We may need it if we don't catch him before she wakes up. Maybe she saw him, or someone else. I still don't think Norgis acted alone." Though he had to admit he hadn't smelled anyone else aside from humans mixed with Norgis' trails.

"Beltar will be thrilled to have a human in his space," Samson mumbled. "Do you need assistance getting her underground?"

"No, I can handle her. You should see if you can follow Norgis' scent from here."

"And what of the mess? The humans will think she was murdered and kidnapped. Not that they would be wrong," he mumbled the last, and Ian shot him a glare.

"Let the humans think what they will." Ian stood, cradling her in his arms, and strode out of the building, leaving Samson to follow the beast. He knew it was his job, knew he shouldn't be abandoning the search for anything, but that didn't matter. All that mattered right now was her. He had to keep her safe, she had to survive. He couldn't imagine living without her now that he'd found her.

It was more difficult to move through the city unnoticed with her than by himself. He had to take a less direct route that kept him away from the busier parts of the city and deeper in the shadows. He managed, however, and when he made it to the entrance of the bunker, Beltar was standing there, waiting for him.

"Move, I have an injured."

"An injured human?" He hissed. "Why would you bring that here, covered in blood? Did you—"

"No! I did not! This is the result of Norgis looking for something at the museum and we need her alive to tell us what he took, or what he's looking for." He was starting to get pissed that everyone assumed he was an uncontrollable monster.

Beltar sniffed the air and frowned. "You gave her your blood."

Ian hissed, "Who are you to question me?"

"I am in charge here. You may be in charge in Atlantis, but this is my territory, Ian, and I have worked hard to prevent *accidents* like this. We don't kill humans and we certainly don't nurse them back to health."

"We need her alive and talking," Ian insisted.

"And what do you plan to do with her after she gives you that information? Throw her out on the street with an erased memory, or let her walk around with knowledge of monsters?"

Ian lifted his chin and gritted his teeth; he had no intention of doing either of those things. "I will do what I need to do when the time comes," he said, careful not to answer the question directly.

"She is your responsibility. Anything that happens to her from here is on your head." Beltar's blue gaze darted to the woman with worry. "I suggest you clean her up before the others return."

"Samson is tracking Norgis from the museum," Ian added, as if that made his decision to bring her here instead of going after the monster himself any better.

"Good, hopefully we can end this tonight, but don't think you'll be returning to Atlantis and leaving us to clean up this mess for you." Beltar pointed a finger at the woman and Ian barely held back a hiss. As if he would ever consider leaving her in the hands of another.

Ian managed a nod of agreement, then rushed inside with her, straight to the room he'd used. He knew the risk of a blood covered human in a small space with so many vampires, so he stripped off her ruined clothing, his hands shaking as he revealed her battered skin beneath. He wanted to go out and kill Norgis with his bare hands right then, but knew he had to be here, had to take care of her first, then he would join the search. He would avenge his woman.

Every inch of her was beautiful, delicate, and perfect, and his soul came to life as he looked down at her form. He ached to touch her, but held himself back. The door opened behind him, and he turned with a growl, crouched and ready to defend.

"I brought water, rags, and bandages," Beltar said, ignoring Ian's threatening stance. "I'll remove the soiled clothing; it will help with the smell of fresh blood in here." He paused, picking up the pile and sniffed. "Was there another there with her?"

"I didn't sense anyone else. What do you smell?" Ian's mind flitted to the look on Samson's face when he'd taken an intentional sniff of the woman. What was he missing, he wondered?

"Nothing, it's probably just your blood mixed with hers and Norgis." Beltar left with the bundle of bloody clothes and Ian turned back to her.

He washed her body clean of blood and dirt, carefully assessing each scratch and bruise. He rebandaged her neck, and bandaged her arm. They were healing quickly but still required a cover. Her leg was badly broken, and he gritted his teeth as he set the bone, knowing he was causing her great pain in the process. She barely made a sound, and that was somehow worse. He would have preferred her to scream out, show that she was alive and well. All he got was a whimper. He splinted the leg so it would heal straight, his hands shaking a bit as he tried not to think about how close he was to her and how naked she was.

He was nearly done, washing her other leg when his hands stilled on her upper thigh, his fingers tracing around a small brown mark, it was a circle with a triangle inside and a bolt of lightning crossing both.

The symbol of Atlantis.

Ian straightened and backed away, staring down at her in disbe-

THE VAMPIRES OF ATLANTIS

lief. He inhaled then with intention, searching through the scent

lief. He inhaled then with intention, searching through the scent of her blood, past the scent of Norgis, the other vampires who lived here and himself. He found what he was looking for, deeply rooted in the core of what she was, a Descendant of Atlantis. His eyes shot to her face, and he wished more than ever that she would wake, that he could demand answers from her. Why was she here and did she know what she was?

Beltar must have smelled it on her, Samson too, that is what had given them pause. This changed everything, and yet, nothing. He quickly covered her with a blanket and took the soiled rags and bloody water from the room. She was his, and it almost made more sense to him now why he was so inexplicably drawn to her. She was always meant to be his.

Beltar was sitting outside the bunker when Ian came out with the rags and water to dispose of. He looked thoughtful and Ian wondered if he'd figured it out too.

"I think she will be fine in a day or two. I will see to all of her needs until then, there is no need for any other to enter that chamber."

"I will see to it that the others know," Beltar assured him. "I will not allow you to keep her against her will, though. If she awakens and wants to be released, you must follow her wishes. Preferably with no memory of all this."

Ian nodded grudgingly; he would do no such thing.

Beltar sighed, "I heard from Samson. He trailed Norgis to a lake and lost the trail there. He could be traveling through underground water tunnels. It will take time to search them all."

"It would be better if we had an idea of what he plans."

"We will figure it out. He's not smarter than any one of us," Beltar scoffed.

"I worry for the humans. Has there been any talk we need to worry about. Strange deaths?"

"Only the one," Beltar said, indicating the bunker. "She's going to be a huge loose end."

Ian just grunted and went back inside.

When he returned to sit beside the woman's bed, his body was tense, and his mind was full. He watched her chest rise and fall all night and it calmed him.

He heard the murmur of voices just before dawn. The others had returned and Beltar was explaining the situation. None disturbed him, and he was grateful. Only when he was certain that they'd all gone to their beds for the day did he strip down and crawl into the bed beside her. Being near her was exhilarating, but he managed to force his body into relaxation and take his day's rest. He would need his strength if he was going to search for the monster when night fell.

As much as he'd like to stay with her, he knew he was duty bound to search. He also desired revenge for the harm that Norgis had done to her, for that the monster deserved a horrific death. So as long as she was safe and not close to waking, he'd do what he could to find Norgis when the sun set.

Five

~~✦~~

WHEN THE SUN SET, Ian woke, stiff from trying to sleep next to her without disturbing her. He didn't move immediately, staring at her as she continued to sleep. Her color was still pale, but improved, and the sound of her heart seemed stronger tonight. He wanted to check her wounds, but that would mean exposing blood and he didn't want to do that until the others had gone out.

He slipped from the bed and adjusted the blankets around her, then dressed and grabbed his weapons. If all went as planned, he would get to destroy the thing that had harmed her. When she woke, he would be able to tell her that he had avenged her, and she would throw herself into his arms in thanks.

If she didn't run from him screaming because he was a monster too.

The thought scared him, and he left the room wishing he could whisk her away to Atlantis before she woke up. Seeing Samson standing across the hall with arms crossed and a scowl on his face had him thinking it was actually a really great plan.

"I can smell her," he hissed.

"Well then, leave," Ian hissed back.

"Beltar put me on guard duty."

"Why the hell would he do that?"

"Because I'm the only one not interested in fucking the human in the bunker," Samson spat and walked away.

Rage boiled in Ian, and he sought out Beltar. "What the hell are you thinking, leaving Samson to watch her?"

"I am thinking that he would rather be anywhere else than in charge of a wounded human woman, and so he is the least likely to disturb her. The rest of us are hunting Norgis."

Ian hated that Beltar was right, but knew it was true. Samson hadn't had the same upbringing as the rest of them. Hadn't been raised by a strong, loving family with the intention of becoming a vampire, an honored position. Samson had come to them much later, saved from horrific slavery. He held on to a hatred of humans because of it, particularly women. Ian had never gotten the full story, but he knew enough. Samson would rather put a stake through his own heart than interact with her. "Fine, let's go."

They started their search at the lake where Samson had tracked the beast.

"Do you smell that?" Laric said as he sniffed around the edge. "Smells like he hopped out here and wasn't alone."

Ian moved to his friend's side and sniffed as well. What he smelled filled him with a deep anger. "Jovi," Ian hissed. His brother, and not just his brother in arms as he considered the others, this was his blood brother. Jovi had defected to above the waterline five hundred years ago, after their father had died and left Ian in charge. Jovi was the older son, but he was too unpredictable, too radical in his beliefs, so their father had chosen Ian as his successor. This was just another sign that their father had chosen correctly.

"Do you think he's behind this?" Laric asked with disbelief.

"Did you know he was in the city?" Ian accused Beltar.

"No! I would have told you straight away if I'd known, and you would have smelled him in the city yourself. He must have just come; we watch our borders carefully. No vamps, no weres, no Descendants, and no Aristotles," Beltar said firmly.

Ian nodded at his friend; he trusted his words. This was the gateway to Atlantis, and its protection was a serious job. Beltar was capable, but not infallible. Ian had to admit neither was he, otherwise Norgis wouldn't even be here, and that knowledge kept him from lashing out at Beltar for this slip.

Jovi should be dead, another thing that was Ian's fault. He'd let his brother go that day, thinking he'd slink away, maybe crawl back eventually. Ian hadn't had it in him to kill Jovi at the time, so deep in grief at the loss of his father. He'd thought, *what real threat could one vampire be?* If Jovi had started making waves on land, Ian would have heard about it. He would have come up with an army and destroyed him, would have covered the right tracks to keep their secret.

He should have expected something like this though, his brother had always been the sneaky type and he was never going to stop trying to rule.

"We need to know what they took. The woman may not wake for another day or two, but there are others at the museum, they might know something by now," Beltar pointed out, no doubt trying to prove he was still in control here.

"We can check it out. Interacting with humans is our specialty," Prat said motioning to Trenton.

"Good," Beltar agreed, and the two took off at a fast pace back toward the city. "We will follow this trail and see what we can figure out. Laric, start tracking, we'll follow."

Laric nodded and took off in the opposite direction. Ian moved to follow Laric, but Beltar reached out a hand and stopped him. Ian looked at him with a questioning eyebrow.

"Tell me, what is your brother after here? What do you know?" Beltar demanded.

Ian stiffened, wanting to snap at Beltar for demanding anything of him, but he knew they needed to work together and

Beltar was the experienced warrior above the waterline. Ian sighed heavily, choosing to ignore the disrespect that was in Beltar's demand. A squabble over control would not aid in their search. "What he's always been after, power."

"Should we call in backup?"

Ian thought about that. Jovi was strong and so was Norgis, but in a fight one on one with either, Ian felt confident. He just didn't expect Jovi to create a fair fight scenario. He couldn't take the two on himself, but he had Beltar's coven to back him up. Two against six, they'd win no problem. "No, we should be able to handle them."

"If it's just the two," Beltar said with a frown.

"No one else escaped," Ian said with surety. "We need more information though," Ian agreed and started to follow Laric. The possibility that Jovi had created himself an army in the last five hundred years was terrifying and very real. The only thing keeping Ian from sliding down that trail of thought was the fact that an army of vampires created a lot of havoc and likely wouldn't go unnoticed. Nothing had been reported to him so he had to hope his brother hadn't gone to those lengths, had to hope that his brother was so over-confident in his own abilities and plan, that he wouldn't think to need more than himself and Norgis.

The trail led them around seemingly nowhere and then back to the museum, but not inside. Ian grew frustrated as it became obvious Jovi had intentionally led them on a random path. Jovi knew they were onto him, and that couldn't be good.

When they got to the museum, Prat and Trenton's scent was strong, they were still there. Had that scared Jovi and Norgis off? Or had the twins come after?

"Wait here," Ian ordered, then strode forward. There was a uniformed police officer standing guard at the back door. The last time Ian had walked through that door he'd, seen something horrific, and something that he hoped never to see again. He took a steadying breath to push the memory aside and smiled at the portly officer.

"Good evening, sir. What are you guarding this night?"

"Nothing for you to worry about, move along," he huffed.

Ian just smiled and caught the man's gaze with his own. He reached through that connection and caught the man's pliable human brain. "You'll let me pass and you won't even see me."

The officer nodded with mouth gaping.

Ian walked around the man and into the building. At first, all he could see was the horror of last night. The blood and carnage, his small woman lying in a heap. Ian shook off the remembered terror and looked with fresh eyes. No one was in this part of the museum. There was blood still on the floor and it was obvious that the human police had been here, gathering evidence of a crime. He heard voices farther in the building and he recognized Prat's, and a human woman was with him.

Ian followed the voices and found Prat with his head buried in a woman's neck.

"I hope you are getting information and not just indulging," Ian said casually, ignoring the delightful smell of fresh human blood. It was nothing compared to his woman's and that made it easy to pass up. Nothing would ever compare.

"Trenton is in charge of information. I'm in charge of indulgence," Prat said, pulling away and smiling. His mouth bloody, and so was the woman's neck. Her eyes were closed, and she was breathing heavily. Her short black hair was pushed to the side, revealing multiple bite wounds from Prat. Ian knew they would be nothing within hours, healed and unless you had the senses of a vampire, unrecognizable. Ian remembered her; she'd been standing near his woman that first night on the street.

"Don't harm her," Ian said, wondering if they were friends. He didn't want to give his woman any more reason to hate him.

"I never harm them, I love them!" Prat said with a seriousness Ian didn't think he was capable of.

Ian could only shake his head. "Norgis was by here. Did you smell him when you got here, or did he come and leave because he smelled you two?"

"He had already passed when we arrived," Trenton said, coming into the room with a book in his hands. "From the smell, he passed near but didn't enter."

"What's that?"

"Notes on what may have been in the destruction. Seems the museum was cataloguing remains from a shipwreck off the coast of the Bahamas. It was French and five hundred years old."

Ian wasn't sure that meant anything, but he tucked the information away for further thought. "Keep searching here. We're tracking Norgis and Jovi."

"Yes sir," Prat said and went back to the woman's neck.

"Don't kill anyone, for fuck's sake," Ian ordered again.

"We know better," Trenton assured Ian.

Ian wasn't reassured, but he walked back out. What had they stopped here for, if it wasn't to come in? Did it mean they'd found whatever it was they'd been after in the first place? Perhaps when they had nearly killed his woman? He didn't have answers, and it really pissed him off. Something told him they were being teased, thrown off the trail, and that meant Jovi had a plan that was far bigger than letting Norgis free for a little destruction.

"They came and left before the twins had shown up, which probably means they have what they were looking for," Ian told Beltar and Laric when he rejoined them.

"Well then, let's see where they went next. Maybe it'll give us a clue," Beltar said with a frown.

The trail circled the building where Ian knew the woman lived, but again it didn't go inside. Were they looking for her?

"What is this place?" Laric asked, obviously noticing the scowl on Ian's face.

"The woman, I believe she lives here," Ian answered grudgingly.

"Were they checking to see if she lives?" Beltar wondered aloud.

"Perhaps," Ian gritted out. He didn't like this, not at all. His instincts were telling him to grab her and go back to Atlantis, to hide her and know that she was safe. But he couldn't do that and still do his job. "Where the hell did they go next?" he hissed.

They followed the trail as it left the woman's apartment building, straight to the entrance to the bunker. This was a terrifying development, but they could tell the two hadn't entered the safe place and they quickly moved on from it.

The trail led to another lake, and that's where they lost it.

"Fuck," Laric hissed as they realized it was useless to keep searching.

"They know where we are, they know about the woman, and they are purposefully showing off," Ian hissed as they made their way back to the bunker.

"We will move to another safe place for the day. We'll cover our trail now that we know we have someone other than humans to hide from, and make a plan," Beltar said. His reasonable tone made Ian want to scream.

"You have somewhere in mind?" Ian gritted out.

"We have a couple safe places throughout the city in case we can't make it all the way back here. They just aren't as spacious or comfortable."

"Great," Ian grumbled, thinking of his tiny human woman.

"Thank fucking god you guys are back," Samson said as they entered the bunker.

"What's wrong?" Ian demanded. He shot an accusing glare at Samson, his mind going to every horrid thing that could have happened to her while he was gone. He'd rip Samson's throat out if he had touched her.

"Nothing except I'm stuck in a hole with a bleeding human," Samson hissed.

"She shouldn't still be bleeding," Ian worried. His blood

should have taken care of the worst of her wounds by now. "Maybe I should give her more."

"Not without feeding yourself," Beltar warned. "Have you eaten since you got here?"

"No," he admitted, but he didn't want to, didn't want anything but her blood, and he couldn't take it while she was still so ill.

"We don't have time now," Beltar said. "We have to go to a safehouse, where is Prat and Trenton?"

"We are here!" They called, coming in smelling like blood and sex.

Ian sneered at the two. They were out of control. He shot a look of disgust at Beltar. He was in charge of them. He needed to get them under control or send them back to Atlantis to mature.

"We are moving out. Grab what you must," Beltar ordered, ignoring the look.

It was an easy task for Ian. He walked into the room where the woman slept and scooped her up. He needed nothing else. He wrapped a blanket around her for warmth and modesty, and he was ready. He took a moment to sniff her, not getting even a hint of Samson. He'd let the vampire live, for now. He breathed deeply the scent of her, mixed with his own and it made his body relax, his mind settle, and every instinct he had in that moment told him to keep her, keep her close, keep her safe, and make her his in every possible way.

His body reacted to that last thought, and he was thankful for the fall of the blanket to cover his erection pushing at his leather kilt as he left the room.

The others were quickly ready as well, carrying small packs. "Do I need my blow-up doll?" Prat asked as they started out of the bunker.

"Gods no," Samson grumbled.

"But Ian's got one," Trenton said with a laugh.

Beltar punched his arm before Ian could attack. Really only

the fact that he didn't dare set the woman down saved Prat from Ian's fist going through his face and knocking out his fangs. Prat just laughed as they headed back out into the night.

"He's a little touchy," Trenton whispered to his brother. "Perhaps the little human tastes sweet."

"I will kill you both and not blink an eye," Ian hissed and got a grunt of agreement from Samson.

"No, you won't, Ian," Beltar snapped. "Prat and Trenton will shut their fucking mouths and once we are settled you should feed. Ian, you cannot help her if you are so weak that you'll attack her." Beltar took a calming breath. "Prat and Trenton haven't killed anyone since they joined me and just because they found a way to enjoy this godforsaken life, doesn't mean they should be punished," he added, mostly to Samson, who was glaring silently.

"I know I need to feed," Ian gritted out and strode forward. "But I still might kill them."

"Oh, come on Ian, you were young once, too," Laric said, trying to ease the situation.

"Yeah, about a million years ago," Ian agreed.

Six

THEY CRISSCROSSED THE AREA, split up, and met back up in an effort to muddy their trail, then headed into the city, which surprised Ian. Beltar led them to a large building that smelled of many humans.

"What is this place?"

"Factory, but it's been abandoned for quite a while. Now it mostly serves as a party place for young humans. There's a basement that's light tight and locks from the inside. We'll be safe there until the sun goes down."

"Cold and damp, that is no place for her to recover!"

"All of our homes are cold and damp. We're vampires, not goddamn humans," Samson snarled and pushed past him.

Ian snarled back and Beltar stepped between the two. "Cool your shit, both of you. Ian, your human will be fine. There are blankets and cots below. If you go feed, then you can come back and give her more blood, which will also aid in the healing. But the sun is not far from up, so it's now or never. No time for fang measuring contests."

Ian wanted to argue, but he knew Beltar was right. He pushed forward and followed Samson down a stairway and through a

46

heavy door. The room was barely big enough for the five cots. It was going to be a difficult day with everyone in there. He pushed a cot into a far corner, as far as he could get from the others, which wasn't much, and laid the woman down. "I can't believe I don't know your name," he whispered.

"Katherine," Prat said casually.

"What?" he hissed at Prat.

"Her name is Katherine. The girl at the museum told me all about her. They think she's dead of course."

Ian turned back to the pale face framed with black hair. He couldn't help touching her sharp eyebrows and delicate nose, then running his finger to her soft pink lips. "Katherine, I will return, and I will give you what you need."

Ian covered her with all the blankets he could and then left with a hiss to the others to *not fucking touch her.* He knew his time was short, could feel the pressure of the sun about to rise. He would not be able to be picky about his meal.

Ian headed out onto the street and walked swiftly until he heard a noise, a groan in a dark alley, and followed it to a pile of rags that smelled like alcohol. He couldn't keep the disdain from his face as he pulled the drunkard up and wiped away layers of dirt before he bit into the man's neck.

He smelled like shit and his blood tasted heavily of the alcohol he'd consumed. The man was so far gone in his drunken haze, Ian didn't even need to pull his mind and tell him to forget the experience, but when Ian dropped the man to the ground, he left him with a gold coin as payment for blood taken. Ian wasn't an animal.

The coin landed in a slice of moonlight and caught his attention. The circle with a triangle in it and a lightning bolt through the middle. The symbol of Atlantis, the symbol he'd seen on Katherine. Did she know what she was? Was that the only reason her blood smelled so sweet to him? Was it why his blood hadn't healed her as much as it should have? Did Beltar know about her? Did the other Descendants know about her?

He could answer that last one with a definitely not. If the Descendants of Atlantis knew one of theirs was out here alone in vampire territory, there's no way they wouldn't have come for her.

A noise at the end of the alley had him startling and hurrying away. It was risky to stay out any longer.

When he arrived back at the basement safe room, the other vampires were laying on cots except for Laric, who had apparently drawn the short straw and was laid out on the floor since Katherine was on the fifth bed. They were all silent, staring up at the ceiling. Ian locked the door and went to Katherine's side. He tore into his arm and pressed it against her mouth. This time she didn't need any prompting. She drank automatically, and her face filled with a delightful pink hue. When she stopped, he pulled away and stared at her. He wanted nothing more than to see her eyes open, but she remained incredibly still except for the steady rise and fall of her chest.

"It doesn't make sense," Beltar said from across the room. "I wonder if Norgis' venom is keeping her from healing?"

Ian hadn't considered that. A poison from the monster could be the problem. "You're probably right. The new blood should help though, and I can smell that her wounds have finally closed."

"We are all thankful for that," Samson grumbled.

"Fuck you," Ian hissed and laid down on the floor next to the cot.

Throughout the day she made little movements and every time she did, Ian startled awake and checked on her. She never woke, but the movements were a good sign. His blood was healing her now, he was sure. It was a long day with little rest for him.

Groans from Prat every time Ian got up to adjust Katherine's blankets were met with snarls from Trenton about his need for beauty sleep. Ian wanted to kill them both, but he managed to ignore them and tend to her. She was all that mattered.

. . .

The pawnshop was open twenty-four hours, and Brandon wasn't at all surprised to see a homeless drunk stumble in with the sun. He smelled like shit, and he was so pale Brandon wondered how he was managing to walk.

"What can I do for you?" He asked cautiously, worried he'd be having to call an ambulance, which was *not* how he wanted to spend the last few hours of his shift.

"What will you give me for this?" The drunk held up a gold coin as he continued to shuffle forward.

Brandon recognized the strange symbol on the coin immediately and sucked in a breath. "Where did you get that?"

"Found it next to me when I woke up this morning," the drunk said with a shrug and touched his neck where Brandon could see there was a suspicious clean spot and two fading red marks.

Brandon tried to keep himself calm as he went into negotiation mode. No need to let this drunk know he had something that anyone would want. He half closed his brown eyes and ran a hand through his short brown hair, absently thinking he needed to wash it, and maybe get a cut. He was about to become a very important person; he'd like to look it. "I'll give you twenty for it."

The drunk's eyes lit up. "Great!"

Brandon almost felt guilty as he handed the man the bill and took possession of the coin. The man's eyes lit up and Brandon watched him pocket the bill and turn to leave with a little more spring in his step. No doubt he'd be passed out again by noon.

"If you come across any more, I'd love to know where it came from. I would pay double to know who has these."

"I didn't steal it," the man defended.

"Of course not," Brandon said. There's no way this drunk would be able to steal anything from a vampire, of that Brandon was certain. "I'm just saying, it's cool. So if you come across it again, let me know."

The man assured Brandon that he'd do that, then hurried out

the door. Brandon locked the front door and rushed into the back office. He pulled out a locked box and reached under his shirt collar for a key he always wore around his neck. He opened the box and pulled out a drawing of a circle with a triangle inside of it and a lightning bolt going through. He nearly giggled with glee as he compared it to the coin. There was no mistake, this was a coin from Atlantis. "They've arrived!" He picked up the phone and dialed a number he never expected to use.

"Speak," came the soft feminine voice on the other end of the line.

Brandon's upper lip started to sweat. "A coin, a coin from Atlantis," he managed to choke out around a throat threatening to close with excitement.

"You're certain?"

"W-well, yes, it's pure gold and has the symbol. The drunk who brought it in had bite marks on his neck."

There was a sharp intake of breath on the other end of the line, then it went dead.

Brandon hung up. That had been the easy part. His hand shook as he pulled out a gun loaded with silver bullets. He shot off a text, then threw back five bolts and locks to open a door to the basement. His pocket buzzed as he stepped down into the dark. He hated this place, avoided it whenever possible. The beast only needed to be fed once a week and usually he made Glen do it, but Glen wasn't here and the sign they'd been told to wait for had just waltzed into his store. At one time there would have been over thirty people to help. In his father's time it had dwindled to ten and now, it was only him and his cousin, Glen.

A low, vicious growl drifted across the basement.

"Shut up, bitch!" Brandon snapped with false confidence as he stared at the black beast behind her bars, silver chains wrapped around her body. He waved the gun in her direction. "You're finally going to live up to your purpose."

She bared her teeth at him, but she stopped growling.

Seven

WHEN THE SUN WENT DOWN, Prat and Trenton were the last to wake, even as the others started making noise, planning for the night's mission.

"I can't leave her; she's near waking, I can feel it," Ian insisted. There was no way he'd allow her to wake here alone and confused or be attended by another vampire who would no doubt frighten her even more.

"She should wake in her own home then, and we won't be stuck with any explaining that needs erasing later on," Samson argued.

Ian couldn't hold back a snarl in his direction.

"Stop it," Beltar hissed. "Samson, head out, see if you can catch them coming out of the water. Take the idiot twins with you."

Samson kicked the twins, and they all headed out.

"Ian, Samson is right. Take her home and leave her there, if you feel like you need to stand guard outside, do so, but she is better off waking alone and healed than here with us."

The reasonableness of Beltar's words and tone did nothing to ease the ache of loss that began in Ian's stomach. "No, not until we know if she has any information on Norgis or Jovi. What if she can tell us what they were after, or are after? What if she knows their plan? She could be in on it for all we know," Ian said, even though he was sure that last part was a huge stretch.

Beltar frowned. "I will circle back to the bunker and watch, see if they return looking for us. Laric, you crisscross the city, see if you happen across a fresh trail."

Laric nodded and took off.

"She could be useful, could have information, but when she wakes, that's it. You can't keep her after she tells you what she might know."

Ian just stared at him. Beltar had no right to tell him what to do.

"I am just trying to be a reasonable voice, Ian. She's a human and you know she won't like what you are."

"Perhaps," Ian agreed.

Beltar frowned, looking thoughtful, and gave Ian a look that clearly stated he knew there was way more behind Ian's desire to stay with the woman than he was admitting. "But where? This isn't a good place for her to recover, obviously."

"What other safe houses do you have? Something more comfortable?"

Beltar pursed his lips in a scowl. "I know a place."

Ian wrapped Katherine in a blanket and lifted her gently, then followed Beltar out into the city. It was early dark and there were people everywhere, so they had to be extra careful. Sticking to shadows, they worked their way to an apartment building.

Beltar froze in a dark alley, a hiss ripping from his lips. "Do you smell that?"

Ian sniffed deeply, trying to search past the sweet smell of Katherine in his arms. When he caught what had made Beltar freeze, he growled and his grip on Katherine tightened. "Wolf."

"It can't be a coincidence," Beltar hissed and started to move again, even faster this time. "The wolves haven't entered this city in years."

Ian followed, eyes darting around and his nostrils taking in great gulps of air, searching for a sign of a nearby werewolf. Nothing could tear through a vampire like a werewolf, which is why the Aristotle Society had employed their help in their delusional drive to keep the vampires away from the humans, as if they were more of a danger. Werewolves were uncontrolled monsters. They belonged locked away in Atlantis, but they'd been better at lying low, hiding until after Atlantis had sunk. Only then did they reveal their truly feral nature. Ian had always regretted his father's decision not to go back for them, letting them thrive above the waterline, feasting on unsuspecting humans. It astonished Ian that they hadn't taken over. It seemed they were content enough to live in hiding. He could respect that decision at least.

"The others don't know about this place," Beltar said. "I keep it for myself, for when I need to get away," Beltar explained when he stopped in front of an apartment building. "Our close quarters coven isn't always easy to handle," Beltar admitted.

He led Ian around the back of the building and up a fire escape. Beltar opened the window with a key and a lot of prying. It was reinforced and certainly no human would be able to get in. Inside looked like a home. Living room, bedroom, bathroom, kitchen. All decorated comfortably and warm, though a bit sparse. It would be a perfect place to continue nursing her to health and when she woke... Ian shivered thinking about what he hoped to happen then. Would she feel the same attraction he did? Would she welcome him into her arms and her veins?

"You can stay with her here; I'll return with news."

"Thank you, Beltar."

Beltar looked conflicted for a moment, then let out a sigh. "You know what she is, don't you?" Beltar said carefully, finally speaking what his worried glances had been saying.

Ian clenched his jaw and his arms tightened around her small body. "What do you mean?"

"I can smell it on her. I think the others are too young to

remember, except Samson, but he's deep in denial. She's a Descendant."

Ian lifted his chin a notch. "I know."

"Then you also know that if she isn't completely clueless about what she is, she is going to hate you, and she is going to try to destroy you."

Ian's stomach clenched and his heart stopped for a moment. "I know that too."

"I never smelled a clan of Descendants in the area. They wouldn't dare come into my territory, so why she's here, I don't know. I can only guess she doesn't know her heritage."

Ian could only nod. He'd come to the same conclusion.

"You cannot keep her, Ian," Beltar said sadly and slipped back out the window before Ian could respond.

Ian looked down at her face, not so pale tonight, and frowned. "Yes, I can," he whispered.

Ian laid her on the bed and removed the bandages from her neck and arm. The wounds were closed but still pink and looked sore. Her leg was harder to tell how it was healing internally. When she woke, he would ask her if it felt healed.

He wanted to bathe her, wanted to put fresh clothing on her so she would wake feeling refreshed and pretty, but he didn't want to go too far, didn't want her to feel as if he'd taken liberties. He would rather die than violate her. So he sat and watched her sleep, waiting for a sign that she was about to wake.

Katherine hurt all over. She had a terrible taste in her mouth, and she really needed to pee. She sat up slowly, rubbing her eyes, and tried to clear the fog of deep sleep from her brain. She blinked as her eyes cleared and she froze. She didn't recognize where she was, and she was naked. Not only that, despite it being very dark in the room, she could tell someone was watching her. It was the beginning of a horror story she had no doubt, if she survived whatever this was, she was never going to be the same.

She screamed and scrambled off the bed as every possibility of horrors that must have already befallen her filled her mind. She tried to drag the blanket with her to cover her body, but she tripped immediately and fell flat on her face. Tears stung her eyes as she waited for the coming attack.

"Katherine!" a deep male voice hissed. "Dammit, are you alright? You shouldn't be out of bed."

"Where the fuck am I, and who the hell are you?" she shouted, hoping to alert a neighbor. Her hand went to her throat, her voice was hoarse, and it hurt a bit to talk. He must have already abused her severely. She cowered on the floor, trying to protect her body with her arms and the blanket.

He didn't approach, but called softly from where he stood across the room. "You're safe, I swear. I am Ian."

She wasn't reassured. Nothing about this felt safe. "I don't know you, Ian," she whispered.

He came to her side then and knelt beside her but didn't touch. "Not yet, no. But I am not going to harm you, I have been caring for you." He reached out, and she allowed him to help her up with gentle hands. "You're safe now."

"Safe can mean a lot of things," Katherine grumbled as he guided her back to sit on the bed. She had a death grip on the blanket around her body, eyes darting around for clothing and trying to think back to what was the last thing she remembered. Had she been assaulted by this man?

He took a step back, giving her space, and she appreciated that. "It was necessary for me to bring you here to heal," he said quietly.

Heal? A new panic welled up inside her as memories flooded through her. "Oh my god," she whispered, it hadn't been him, and it hadn't been a sexual assault. It had been something even more unimaginable. "The thing, it, it smelled so bad, and it oozed into the room and it, it was going to kill me!"

"Yes, Norgis, that is why you're here now. I healed you; I swear that I only did what was necessary to heal you, I took no liberties."

Katherine shook her head, trying to get rid of the memories. Weeping green skin, flaming red hair and bright red eyes. The thing had sharp claws and teeth and when it spoke, its breath smelled like death. She'd been alone in the museum storage, was trying to make order out of the chaos left of her work. She wasn't sure how it had gotten in, but it moved quickly for its awkward, bulky shape.

"Can you turn on a light please," she whispered, not wanting to be stuck in the dark with a stranger again.

"Of course," he said in a tone that made her think he was just happy she wasn't screaming or running away.

The light came on and she had to blink a few times to adjust. When she did, she gasped. Standing before her was quite possibly the most beautiful man she'd ever seen. He was tall and broad, with pale skin and blond hair pulled back into a ponytail. His eyes were a brilliant sea green, and they watched her carefully. He was wearing a black t-shirt and what looked like a leather kilt. Was that a sword hanging from his belt?

"Ian?" she asked carefully.

"Yes, I am Ian," he said with a smile that made her heart skip a beat.

She looked down at herself and bit her lip. What skin was exposed outside the blanket was dirty and she shuddered to think of what her hair and face must look like. She touched her leg where it was tied to a couple of sticks. That was what had made her trip getting out of bed. What all had happened to her? She was thankful that the memories stopped at the approach of the monster. Her mind knew she couldn't handle the details.

"It was broken. It should be healed now though, also your neck and arm were damaged."

She touched her throat. That made sense why her voice hurt. "Can I get some water?"

"Yes!" he said excitedly and rushed out. He was back moments later with a cup of water.

She drank greedily, and it did a lot to soothe the ache in her throat. "Shit, how long have I been out?" Her mind started to spin around her life, her job, and friends. What did people know. What did they think?

"A couple of days."

Katherine did a slow blink and raised her eyes to meet his. "A couple days... and a broken bone healed?" She was no medical expert, but that was impossible, she was certain. Then again, the monster that attacked her was impossible too, so she had to admit, she didn't know everything.

He looked uncomfortable and stiffened. "Are you hungry? I can bring you whatever it is you need."

That distracted her. She wasn't hungry, but she needed a bathroom in the worst way. "Can you remove this splint so I can use the bathroom?" she asked, embarrassed. She didn't want to risk letting go of the blanket and untying the splint would definitely require two hands. It didn't occur to her to ask him to leave so she could do it herself. Apparently, she'd decided he wasn't the threat she'd assumed he was at first.

"Of course!" He moved swiftly, too swiftly, to her side, making her jump a little. "Sorry, I didn't mean to frighten you." His voice was low and careful, as if he were holding back things he wanted to say, and it made her nervous.

She watched him cautiously as he removed the bandages from her leg with gentle movements. There was something very frightening about him and something so attractive at the same time. She was worried she was about to start drooling as she eyed the way his muscles moved under the tight shirt and how the light shone off his long hair. It looked so soft she wanted to touch it. She was probably losing her mind, she decided, as he moved away, the attack had addled her brain. "What was the thing that attacked me?"

"Its name is Norgis. It is a monster that was being held prisoner in Atlantis. I tracked him here and I am sorry I was too late to keep him from attacking you. I'll never forgive myself for that." He met her gaze and there was a deepness there that made her gasp. "I vow to never let another thing harm you, Katherine. I would rather die myself than see you harmed by anything."

She gulped; his intensity was overwhelming. "A—you—um, okay," she didn't know how to respond to any of what he'd just said, but his seriousness and the fact that she'd seen the thing with her own eyes had her believing his words against her better judgment. It hadn't been human, and it was unlike any animal in existence and looking at him told her there was something a little more than human there, too. No man looked like that or talked like that, and it hit all of her yummy buttons. She bit her lip to keep her mind off of the close proximity and her nakedness. Was it too soon for Stockholm Syndrome?

"I will explain everything, I promise."

"Okay, but first, where's the bathroom?"

"Shall I carry you there?"

"No!" she said forcefully, and her face heated. She wasn't sure what he'd done or seen in the last couple of days, and she had a pretty good idea that he'd already seen her everything since she was nude, but that didn't mean she wanted him to carry her around or help her in the bathroom.

He smiled and pointed to the door. "The living area is there and through that is a bathroom."

Katherine got up slowly, testing her leg and balance, it felt great, maybe it hadn't been broken, only bruised. Still clutching the blanket, she started to move out of the room. "I need clothes," she said with a sigh.

"Of course, I'll find something."

She didn't fall as she shuffled to the door and out to the living room, which was sparsely furnished with a couch, chair, and table. A door stood open showing the bathroom, and she headed for it wondering if this is where he lived. She somehow doubted it. It was far too impersonal, looked more like a hotel room than someone's home. So where the hell were they? Was she even still in Miami? She let her brain touch on the fact that he'd mentioned *Atlantis*. That wasn't a real place... Right?

She flipped on the bathroom light and closed the door, locking it, even though she doubted it would keep him out if he wanted in. He was inhumanly huge and muscled. She would be a little more freaked out by that fact if she hadn't always felt like there was more to the world than most people thought. She just never believed she would come face to face with anything that lurked in the dark.

She looked into the mirror and groaned. Her hair was a disaster, her face was bruised, and her neck looked like it had survived a dog bite, but just barely survived it. She really hoped the scars would fade, then she was overwhelmed by the realization that the wound that would have left those scars had to have been life threatening. How the hell had she survived? And without a hospital stitching her up? She looked at her arm, it too was deeply scarred and still sore. She remembered raising it to defend herself as the thing had approached. Its huge black claws had burned as they sunk through her skin like it was butter.

She was lucky to be alive, and if Ian was telling the truth, she owed him her life.

Tears threatened to overwhelm her, and she decided she would indulge in a quick shower to ease her nerves before she started asking *a lot* of questions.

She cursed as she wrapped herself in a towel after her shower, but she had no other option. She found a brush and ran it through her tangled hair and was happy with the result. She didn't look like she'd been dragged through hell anymore, so it was an improvement. When she left the bathroom, she found Ian sitting stiffly on the couch with a frustrated look on his face and a sword by his side.

"Um, is everything okay?" she asked, darting her gaze between the sword and his face.

"Yes, fine," he grunted, not making her feel like it was fine at all. "How are you feeling? You should rest."

"I feel surprisingly well, though I wish I had clean clothes, did you find anything? Then I want answers," she said with a confidence she didn't really feel, but she knew she didn't want to present herself as a pushover. Whatever this situation was, she wanted to come out of it alive and she didn't know if she could trust him fully yet.

Ian indicated a pile on the chair. "It was all I could find. I'm sorry it isn't better."

Katherine picked up a large men's t-shirt and a pair of sweats, also for a man about Ian's size. "Do you live here?"

"No."

"Are these yours?" she asked, holding up the clothing.

"No."

She sighed at his clipped answers and went back into the bathroom. He was not exactly chatty. The t-shirt would work, baggy though it was, but the sweats were ridiculous so she decided to go with just the shirt. At least it reached almost to her knees, though if she had underwear, it would be even better. Self-conscious and trying to ignore it, she left the bathroom once more and sat on the chair, curling her legs under her and pulling the shirt down to cover as much as she could. She felt like a toddler wearing dad's shirt and wondered what he thought of her.

Ian just watched her with indiscernible intensity. His eyes didn't leave her for a second and it was unnerving and exciting at the same time. No one had ever watched her that closely.

Once she stopped fussing with her shirt, he spoke. "Ask me anything."

"What's with the sword? Am I a prisoner?"

"No!" he said with genuine shock. "It is for your protection."

"Okay, protection from the thing that attacked me before."

"Among other things, yes."

When he didn't proceed to tell her what those other things were, she sighed heavily. "Okay, so now would be a good time to start telling me everything."

"First, I must know, do you recall what Norgis was after, when he came to the museum? What was he seeking, and did he find it?"

Katherine frowned and tried to remember. "I was looking through the rubble and had just found a small box from a shipwreck that was recently brought in. A Spanish ship had gone down near the Bahamas about five hundred years ago and they had just brought up a bunch of items. I was in the middle of cataloguing all of it when the teenagers decided to come in and make a mess of things." She gritted her teeth, still angry over the unnecessary destruction. "It wasn't kids, was it," she asked him.

"It was Norgis," he said with a nod.

"The box I found had been rusted shut when I'd seen it the first time, but because of the destruction, it had cracked the seam, and I was able to open it." Katherine paused as the memory solidified. Her hands had been shaking as she'd moved the lid and peered inside. She'd felt a tingle over her entire body looking into the box. It was something no one had laid eyes on in five hundred years, and she was getting to see it first! It was thrilling, the type of thing she imagined doing as a kid, digging up artifacts in a jungle like Indiana Jones.

"What was in there?" Ian prompted.

Katherine met his gaze. "A small green stone with a mark on it."

"A circle with a triangle and a lightning bolt through it?" Ian guessed.

"Yes, just like my—" Katherine stopped and bit her lip. No, that couldn't be anything.

"Just like the birthmark on your thigh," Ian finished for her.

Her face flamed, knowing he'd gotten up close and personal enough to see the thing. "Yes."

"Shit!" Ian hissed and stood angrily.

Katherine flinched back and watched him pace through the small space. His anger intimidated her, but her curiosity always got the better of her. It was the reason she had become an archivist. Everything ancient fascinated her and whatever had been in that box must have been important.

"What is it? What does it mean?" she pressed.

"It means you are in great danger, even more so than before," he hissed angrily.

Katherine bit her lip and tried to be calm. "Okay, so what now?"

Ian stopped pacing and turned to look at her fiercely. "I have to tell the others what we are up against."

"Others?"

"Yes." He took a deep breath and fell to his knees, bowing his head. "Katherine, I am a vampire."

Loud, nervous laughter erupted from her at his words. "Vampire?" she said with a shake of her head. She was willing to believe in the boogey man, he'd attacked her, but vampire? She let her eyes trace over him. He was huge, but lots of men were. He was pale, and this *was* Miami. He was fast in his movements, and he'd somehow healed her within days of being viciously attacked. But vampire?

Ian lifted his head and looked offended. "You don't believe me?"

"Actually, I think I do," she said with a nervous laugh. "And that's what is so ridiculous. I was attacked by a monster that looked like swamp thing. I know I nearly died because the scars left behind are horrendous. I was only healing for a couple days, and here I wake up in a dark strange apartment with a man who looks like he belongs on the cover of a romance novel, and he's telling me he's a vampire. It actually makes perfect sense."

Ian frowned. "You are taking this well."

"I'm a scientist. I know that the possibilities of truth are far beyond what most humans accept and until I see proof that you aren't what you say you are, I believe you. Vampires exist, monsters exist, and there's some kind of stone from a five-hundred-year-old shipwreck that has a mark on it that matches my very strange birthmark." She shrugged. Somehow the reality of it all was comforting. She'd always wondered about her heritage. Being adopted left a lot to the imagination so maybe she was finally going to figure it out.

"I need to tell my men what you have told me. It explains a lot and means there is more danger to come."

Katherine nodded. That all seemed to be perfectly sensible too, and she started to worry her mind was snapping. "I need to go home and get clean clothes; I need to call my boss and tell him I'm alive and Jenny! She must be so worried."

"I don't think that's a good idea. You are still very much in danger. It's better if no one knows you are still alive right now."

She tried to look firm as she raised her eyebrow. She had no interest in this man, or vampire, telling her what to do. "You want me to let my friends think I'm missing? No way, that's just cruel."

"They likely think you're dead, with as much blood as there was at the scene," Ian said quietly, trailing off, his eyes darkened.

Katherine shuddered at the look of rage that passed through his eyes. "Well, I'm not staying here, wherever the hell here is," she continued with less conviction. "I don't even have any damn underwear."

"A safehouse in the city."

"Why won't I be safe at my house and why can't I tell people I'm alive?" She demanded, still not believing it was necessary.

"It's best if the monsters think you're dead."

"And my friends? My job?"

"They have already mourned you; do you think that a few more days will matter?"

Katherine was frustrated by his reasonable tone, but she had no reason to think he was lying about the monsters, and she didn't miss the plural there and she shuddered thinking that more than one of those things might be wandering around Miami. At least she could be thankful she didn't have family to worry over her. She had no idea who her father was, and her mother had been a young runaway who died in childbirth. She'd been adopted by a nice family, an older couple who couldn't have kids. They'd both passed a few years ago, leaving her without any family. Jenny was the only one Katherine really cared to talk to and let know that she was alive, but she supposed he was right. A few more days wouldn't matter in the end. Coming back from the dead was an ordeal that could wait.

"Fine, I just want clean clothes," she sighed.

His entire body relaxed at her agreement. "I will get you what you need if you promise to stay here."

"Okay," she agreed, because she wasn't sure she could argue with someone who literally drank blood. Did he drink blood? Was she in danger from him? No, she decided quickly. If he'd been able to help her heal from her wounds, then she wasn't in danger of him trying to suck out all her blood, but she did wonder, and her eyes watched his mouth carefully for a glimpse of fang.

"Don't leave!" Ian hissed as he stood.

"Yes sir," Katherine mocked and let her lips curl into a half smile. Something about him was terribly frightening and at the same time, she wasn't afraid at all. "One thing first."

"Anything," he said so quietly it was almost a breath and somehow that one word sent a shiver down her spine to pool in her belly.

"What does it mean? The symbol, why is it important and why is it on me?"

He sighed and ran a hand through his hair. "That is a long story. I promise I will be back before the sun rises and I will tell you everything you wish to know."

Katherine nodded. "What the hell time is it?" There were no clocks, and the windows were blocked out. She couldn't see anything, but he seemed sure it was dark out.

"It's early morning. There are still a few hours till dawn. You should try to rest now. You're still in need of healing. I'll bring back food when I return as well. I know humans need to eat."

"Oh, yeah, I guess I should eat something. How am I not starving after days of not eating?" she wondered aloud.

"You had my blood. It will suffice as nutrition for a while, I suppose."

"What?" She couldn't help screeching and her stomach turned. She'd *had* his blood! "Oh fuck," she gagged and ran for the bathroom, unloading everything that had been in her stomach, which wasn't a lot and when she glimpsed the color, she clamped her eyes closed and flushed away the evidence before it could trigger more dry heaving.

"Are you unwell?" Ian asked with concern in his voice. He was in the doorway, and she hated that he'd just watched that embarrassing act.

"I guess blood just doesn't agree with me," she snapped and sagged back against the bathtub.

He laughed, and she picked up the garbage can and threw it at him.

"I'll be back soon. Don't leave."

She didn't say anything, just laid her head on the edge of the tub and closed her eyes. She listened to his footsteps move through the apartment and the window shut. She was alone, and she already missed his presence.

Eight

Ian hated to leave Katherine, but he had to tell Beltar what he'd found out. The implications of the Stone being in Jovi's hands was horrifying.

Thankfully, it didn't take long to track them to the entrance of the bunker.

"Ian, does your lady wake?" Laric asked with a smile.

"She does, and she had some information." He gave Beltar a look to indicate how right he was about keeping her.

Beltar just rolled his eyes. "Better than we did, It seems as though Norgis and Jovi stayed hidden this night," Beltar admitted with a grumble.

"And the werewolf?" Ian had crossed more than one trail of its scent as if it were searching the city. A werewolf newly in the city needed to be chased out before it got ideas of making a permanent residence here.

Laric frowned. "We didn't find it, but we did run across its scent mixed with a magic that might be hiding it."

"Aristotle wolves?" Ian hissed.

Beltar shook his head. "One problem at a time. What did you find out from Katherine?"

"They took the Descendants' Stone," Ian hissed, his mind uneased by the werewolf still lurking about.

"How?" Samson demanded.

"I don't know for certain. Katherine said it was in a box that came out of a shipwreck that's been under the sea for five hundred years."

"About the time that Jovi made his break from Atlantis," Beltar mumbled.

"If he took it when he left, but lost it along the way, this is something he's been waiting a very long time for, and his plan will be solid. We need to interfere as soon as possible," Samson said.

"What about the Descendants? We need to warn them, offer them protection," Laric added.

"Yes," Beltar agreed quickly. "Laric, take Samson and go north. Warn them. We'll keep searching here or follow Jovi wherever he heads."

Laric nodded and raced off with Samson to head north.

"How far is the clan of Descendants?"

"Too far for what's left of tonight. It won't be long before they have to take to ground for the day. If they're lucky, they should be able to make contact before tomorrow morning. It won't be easy to locate their settlement," Beltar said with a frown.

"Does this mean we are free to carouse until sunrise?" Prat asked with a wide grin.

"Sure, I don't think there's any use in continuing the search tonight, but keep alert for the werewolf," Beltar said, and the twins took off at a blurring speed.

"You're certain those two are following the rules?" Ian asked with a frown.

Beltar ignored Ian's question. "What do you intend to do with the woman?"

Ian knew what Beltar wanted to hear, but he wasn't going to lie to his friend, and he wasn't going to let her go. "Katherine has agreed to stay hidden in the apartment for now. I will gather some essentials for her and stay with her. I think that it's best if Jovi doesn't think she survived, if he knows what she is..." Ian couldn't finish that thought aloud. It was too terrifying. "Tomorrow night I'll meet you at sunset," Ian's tone dropped, and his hand clenched around the hilt of his sword. "And we hunt. Even if we have to crawl through those watery caves, we will find Jovi and we will stop whatever insanity he plans."

Beltar nodded approvingly and Ian took off. He didn't have much time, so he rushed straight to her apartment building.

He waited across the street for a while, hidden by shadow, making sure it wasn't being watched by one of their police. They had to be investigating her murder by now. He didn't see anyone, so he went forward when a young woman walked to the door with an armload of bags.

"Can I hold the door for you, Ma'am" he said silkily, catching her gaze. "Unlock the door and I'll hold it for you," he said, easily manipulating her mind into doing as he asked. He didn't want to have to break this lock and alert anyone to his presence here.

"Of course," she said dreamily, and quickly unlocked the door. He held it open for her, and she smiled drowsily as she passed.

Once inside, he followed the scent of Katherine up to the third floor and to a door which he had no hesitation in breaking the lock to enter. There he was overwhelmed by the scent of her. It permeated this place. She'd obviously lived here for a while, and alone. He couldn't scent anyone else except for the slightest bit. He wanted to look at everything, to learn about who she was and what she loved, if she loved someone. That thought made him reach for his sword. What if she had someone! But no, the evidence said she lived alone and was rarely visited. It both saddened and delighted him. She deserved to be loved, by him.

He didn't have time to snoop around at all of her things though. The sun was going to rise, and he had to be back with her before then. He stuffed a few things into a bag he found in her closet along with some food from her kitchen and was soon rushing back out of the building, back to her. There was no way he was going to get caught somewhere away from her during the day, but he knew he was cutting it close.

He wasn't paying enough attention to his surroundings, too eager to get back to her, wondering what she was doing right this moment. Was she sleeping, or was she waiting up for him? He didn't sense the slight burn of magic in the air, the whiff of wolf, until it was too late.

A low growl wasn't something he could miss though, alerting him to his mistake.

Ian dropped his bundle and crouched, sword in hand. He faced down the alley outside the apartment where Katherine waited for him, and into the darkness that could hold his death. He could just make out the silhouette of the beast, too small. This wasn't the werewolf he expected to see, and behind it stood a lanky human with wide eyes and a fearful set to his open jaw. The glint of silver in the man's hand told Ian everything he needed to know.

"You mean to challenge me?" Ian asked in a low tone, hoping Katherine wouldn't be alerted to what was going to happen here.

The man walked forward and so did the beast he had on a silver leash. No doubt the leash was enhanced with magic to keep the fresh scent of the beast disguised. Being silver, it would keep the beast weak enough to not escape, to follow commands and not bite the hand that fed it. It was a one-sided relationship, and the beast could earn its dinner by tearing out the throats of vampires. Ian had no empathy for the wolf, even if it appeared to be abused and neglected under the care of the Aristotle Society. He'd never met a werewolf that wasn't trying to rip out his throat, and he had a strong desire to keep living, especially now. His gaze darted up to the closed window and hoped the man didn't notice.

"I am Brandon of the Aristotle Society," the man said with a shaky voice.

"Where is your army?" Ian demanded, expecting to be overrun at any moment. The last time he'd fought one of Brandon's kind it had been an army against an army and Ian's men had suffered greatly, though they'd emerged the victors in the end.

"I don't need an army against one bloodsucker," he said with a little more confidence and raised a gun, aiming for Ian's chest.

"What, no wooden stake?" he laughed

"I'm told a wooden bullet will do," Brandon said with a slight shake to his voice.

Ian frowned. It certainly would do. If the werewolf's fangs didn't rip into him deep enough to bleed him out, a wooden bullet placed right would stop his long life. Fortunately, the shake in the man's hand and the untrained way he held the weapon left doubt in Ian's mind about the validity of the threat. The wolf, however, watched him with deep yellow eyes. Her white fangs shone in the moonlight out of a black face. This was a real threat if the man let her off the leash.

Why wasn't he letting it off the leash? The Aristotle Society used these beasts to do the killing. Never had he encountered an army that relied on the weapons they brought.

Ian's face broke into a wicked smile. "Where is your sire? Who is your teacher?"

The man's hand shook all the more, and the werewolf growled.

Ian took a step forward. "Are you all alone? I've faced armies of your ancestors and yet I am still here. You think to take me down alone and obviously untrained with a malnourished werewolf and a wooden bullet?"

"Others are on their way to the city," he said with a false confidence that Ian didn't believe.

Ian took another forward step, and the man stepped back, landing in the light of a nearby streetlamp. "Brave of you to come out hunting before they arrive."

"Stay back! I'll release her!" Brandon threatened shakily.

Ian glanced at the werewolf as he stepped closer. She was sickly. The fur around her body was thin in patches, almost showing skin and where the silver collar sat against her neck, it was raw. He could now clearly smell the blood under the magic. This was not what he'd expect to see from the Aristotle Society and its werewolves.

"You are alone, untrained, and that beast you have on the chain is as likely to turn and rip out your throat as mine if you let her loose," Ian laughed darkly. "I think you know that. I don't think you'll let her go."

The man's eyes widened with fear and the sound of his finger on the trigger was enough to warn Ian, but not enough for him to get completely out of the way. The bullet lodged into Ian's shoulder. The werewolf pulled against her restraints and the man fell to the ground as he struggled for control.

Ian didn't wait around to see what would happen next. Quick as a flash, he grabbed the bundle for Katherine and disappeared up the side of the building. The human's eyes wouldn't be able to follow where he'd gone. The wolf's would, but he doubted she was interested in chasing him down in her weakened state.

As Ian pulled the window shut, the first rays of daylight licked at his hand. He sucked in a hiss and bit back a curse as his skin singed and smoked.

"What the hell is that smell?" Katherine said, as he turned with his bundle of items for her. "Oh my god! Ian, you're smoking! What the hell happened?"

"It'll stop momentarily. I didn't quite beat the sun," he said, trying to make light of the pain. It was bearable. "This hurts a bit more," he grimaced as he touched his shoulder.

"Fuck! You're bleeding!"

When she rushed to him with concern on her face, he almost wished the injury was more serious. And as she touched him gently and cooed over the red blistering skin of his hand and bleeding shoulder wound, he wished his entire body had been exposed to the light. Just to have her hands on him, caring for him, he'd take the pain of a thousand suns licking across his exposed skin, hundreds of bullets through his flesh to see her eyes look at him as if he were no less human than herself. He couldn't remember a time when a Descendant had looked at him like that, treated him as if he were precious and breakable. It made his heart swell.

"Sit, I'll get some ice and bandages," she said and hurried off, then paused and looked back at him. "Wait, no you need aloe, maybe stitches. I'm not sure I'm qualified for that. Do you need a doctor?" she asked, halfway to the kitchen, which he was certain held no ice anyway. "Is there a first aid kit here?"

Her words were rushed and frantic. He saw panic in her eyes, and he couldn't help laughing as he sat where she'd instructed.

"The only first aid a vampire needs is fresh blood," he said with a sigh, knowing she wasn't about to give him that, but he'd heal quick enough without it. He had all day to wait.

"Oh," she whispered, and her hand went to her neck, her eyes wide and frightened.

He cursed himself for saying anything, but he didn't want her to waste her time worrying about something as silly as stitches and bandages. "Don't worry, it'll heal on its own. I brought you clothing and food." He held out the bags, but her eyes stayed locked on his mouth and he frowned. Was she about to decide she was frightened of him? Was this where she ran away screaming, never to be seen again? He braced himself for it, knowing he couldn't keep her here against her will, it would kill him to do anything that might harm her body or spirit.

"You are the only reason I'm alive," she whispered and walked toward him. "I looked at all my scars while you were out. They had to have been deep wounds and there's no way I would have survived without you. I owe you my life and you have asked for nothing in return." Her eyes locked with his as she knelt in front of him. "Please Ian, let me do this for you." She tilted her head and her hair swept away, exposing her soft neck, still scarred from Norgis. Her hands laid gently on his thighs, warm and delicate.

Ian nearly groaned at the sight of her knelt before him, the word please had nearly been his undoing, he could feel his body hardening, the desire he already held for her was amplified beyond anything he'd experienced before.

"Katherine, you don't have to do this," he whispered as he trailed his finger over the pulsing vein in her neck. More than anything he wanted a taste, had been thinking of it since he'd first scented her in the city. But this offering, it was nothing he could have ever imagined. Without coercion, she wanted to give to him, wanted him to take from her. It was beautiful, and it made his chest ache.

"I want to, Ian. Take what you need. I trust you." Her voice didn't waver, she gave away not an ounce of doubt.

That trust was exactly why he hesitated. He couldn't lose himself with her, couldn't stand to be a monster in her eyes. Even if he didn't kill her, he could so easily scare her, and lose her forever. Now more than ever, he knew he wanted to keep her, forever.

He couldn't deny all of what she was offering so sweetly. He was only a man after all, but he'd be careful. He picked up her hand from where it rested on his thigh and brought her wrist to his mouth. He dragged his tongue over the skin. It would help to dull the bite. "Watch me," he demanded as he spread his lips and exposed his fangs.

Her blue eyes were wide as they locked onto his mouth and her own lips were parted on a gasp. She was so beautiful.

When he bit into her creamy flesh, she jolted from the shock, but didn't pull away and didn't stop watching him. The taste of her hot blood on his tongue was more than he could have hoped for. His entire body thrummed with desire and knowing she watched made it so much better. He could feel her pulse speed up and as he watched, her chest began to rise and fall erratically. For a moment he worried that he was taking too much, but then she sucked in her lower lip, and he knew she was just as turned on by this interaction as he was. His shoulder muscle twitched as the wooden bullet was pushed from his body, and his arm tingled as it healed.

Katherine bit back a groan. Never in her life would she have imagined she'd be turned on by something like this. A goddamn real vampire had his fangs in her wrist, sucking blood from her body, and all she could think about was what he might not be wearing under his leather kilt and how much she wanted to feel those lips on her own.

She shuddered as he licked the punctures and pulled away, all the while his green eyes held hers. She saw a question there that she wasn't ready to answer.

She stood on shaky legs and turned, wanting to bolt for the privacy of the bedroom. She got two steps before she froze. Images exploded in her mind. Every romance novel she'd ever read where the dark dreamy hero lets the beautiful heroine nurse him to health ended with wild sex that always had her reaching for her battery-operated boyfriend. She dreamed many nights of being in similar situations and hadn't she just been telling Jenny about how she wanted to be swept off her feet? What could be more sweeping than a vampire, in nearly any scenario where he wasn't homicidal?

She turned back. He was standing now too, his fists clenched and his face unreadable.

"Ian," she said on a breath, accepting that she was about to do something that she may never be able to recover from. His lips twitched up into a seductive smile and she lost all will to stop herself. She threw herself across the space separating them and he caught her easily, her legs wrapped around his waist and since she was still wearing only the long shirt, her ass was exposed, and his hands were hot on her bare skin. He crushed his lips to hers and she slid her fingers into his soft hair.

His lips worked against hers expertly. She parted her own and his tongue slipped inside to tease and tantalize hers with the taste of—

"Oh shit," she said, scrambling from his arms and racing to the bathroom, where she promptly threw up.

"Katherine! What is it?"

"Not a blood fan," she said with her head against the toilet seat.

His laugh was unexpected, deep and jovial. She glared at him from her spot on the floor. She flushed the toilet and sighed. That wasn't the way her romance novels ended a first kiss. She had ruined a perfectly good opportunity to be swept off her feet.

"You should probably eat something if you are going to keep puking."

"Yeah, you're probably right," she said, standing up, filled with embarrassment. "I guess I'll put some of my own clothes on, too."

He reached out and tucked a lock of hair behind her ear, thoughtfully then trailed his hand down to the neck of the t-shirt. He frowned and his nostrils flared in distaste as he plucked the material gently. "Yes, that is a good idea."

Her face flushed and anger replaced her earlier embarrassment. He had the audacity to think she wasn't looking her best after she'd given him her blood and then he'd kissed her as if he were going to die without her touch. She pushed past him and grabbed her bag, slamming the bedroom door behind her.

"Asshole," she hissed as she started pulling things out of the bag. She didn't find much, no underwear, a couple of dresses that were only appropriate for a night on the town, a pair of jeans, sweats and a couple t-shirts. It looked like he had grabbed and run without thinking. She pulled on the sweats and a t-shirt, then stared at the closed door. Part of her wanted to crawl into the bed and not face him until absolutely necessary. Another part wanted to prove she didn't care what he thought of her appearance. The rumble of her stomach closed the debate.

With head held high. She left the bedroom. She hated it, but she couldn't help smoothing her hair back and hoping she looked alright. He was sitting on the couch when she emerged and stood as soon as she entered the room. His face had a look of concern, and he absently rubbed his chin as he looked her up and down.

"What?" she snapped, hating that her anger was in her tone. She'd have liked to go with cool and uncaring. She hurried to the kitchen where a bag of food sat and tried to take deep breaths.

He followed her with a look of confusion on his face, but she ignored him. She wasn't going to let him play dumb.

"I have offended you," he finally said.

"Ya think?" she grumbled as she dumped the bag on the counter. It was obviously from her kitchen, so luckily it was all things she liked.

"Well, woman, what is it?" he hissed with exasperation.

Katherine looked him straight in the eye, grabbed an apple and took a bite. She chewed slowly and thought about how to respond to his slightly sexist remark. She swallowed and set the apple down.

"How old are you?"

"Is that the problem? I am many years older than you, but you're no young woman yourself. Are you a virgin?" He asked with a disbelieving tone.

Katherine was glad she'd swallowed because she probably would have choked at that question. Her face heated with anger. "Not a virgin and not old, so fuck you."

His eyebrow quirked up at her curse, and his obvious delight made her all the more pissed off. "Well then, what is it?" he asked with an amused tone.

She glared at him and ate another bite, chewing slowly and swallowing before she answered. "I can't help that I was passed out for two days healing from near death and don't have access to makeup," she finally said with a little more emotion than she'd intended, even after taking her time to answer.

Ian cocked his head to the side and looked her up and down again. "I don't see the issue. You look fine."

Katherine threw the apple at him.

He easily dodged it. "Woman, what is your problem?" He asked again, this time he had more than a hint of anger in his voice.

"Fine? I look fine? Five minutes ago, your hands were on my bare ass and then you looked at me like you couldn't stand the sight of me and now I look *fine?*"

Ian laughed and walked around the counter. He pulled her to him and kissed her hard and hot on the mouth. "I would strip you down and fuck you on this counter right now if I thought it wouldn't scare you away, my dear. I only thought it a good idea for you to change because I didn't like the sight and smell of another man's shirt on your naked body. You should bear no one's scent but mine, wear no one's clothes but mine." He growled the last and his lips trailed kisses along her neck. "Mine."

She was shivering when he pulled away, leaving her craving him like a crack addict.

"Now eat, you need to build your strength back up." He pushed the food in her direction with a smirk. He knew what he'd done. His eyes dipped down to her hardened nipples. "Otherwise, you'll never be ready for what I want to do to you."

Ian walked away, and she scarfed down two apples and a granola bar as her mind flipped around his words. *Mine.* It had been spoken with such possessiveness it had sent a shiver down her spine and she wasn't sure how she felt about what that one word might mean. Being swept off one's feet was one thing, but being roped into some sort of forever relationship after a kiss was another.

She felt better after the food, and tired, but she wasn't going to be able to sleep without more answers. She joined Ian on the couch and stifled a yawn.

"Tell me about Atlantis," she said when he didn't immediately start talking.

"That story is long, and you need to rest. Go sleep in the bed. I will guard you all day. You have nothing to worry about."

"And tonight?"

"Tonight, I must join my brothers in a hunt, to make sure you stay safe." He looked like he was struggling with the next words. "And I would ask that you stay here." His words were careful, and he didn't look at her as he said them.

Katherine bit her lip and twined her fingers nervously. "I'm not your prisoner?"

"No," he said with real surprise and locked eyes with her. "Katherine, you are not my prisoner. If you wanted to walk out that door right now, I would not stop you, nor could I with the sun up. But there is a great danger in the city, and I cannot protect you if you leave." There was a heartache behind his words that made her gasp.

Katherine nodded. She believed him, she knew he meant only to keep her safe. She could leave if she wanted to, and that was enough.

As she slipped into the bed and closed her eyes, her mind replayed his words over and over again. *I would strip you down and fuck you on this counter right now if I thought it wouldn't scare you away, my dear.* She couldn't believe how much she wanted that exact thing to happen. The fact that she was sleeping alone only made her crave him harder. Was that his plan? To drive her to distraction with promises of untamed passion? If so, he was an expert at sweeping a girl off her feet.

She was doomed to fall, hard, and she didn't think she cared at all.

Nine

BRANDON THREW the bolt on the cage. "Stupid bitch," he sneered at the now cowering wolf. "You let him get away. What the hell are you even good for?"

She just looked at him with her large yellow eyes, but it was enough to make Brandon shiver. He wondered what would happen if he didn't keep that collar on her all the time. His grandfather had been very specific to never take it off, but she didn't look like she would do much. She looked half dead, and stupid too.

Brandon kicked the bars of the cage. "Next time, you'd better cooperate, or you won't be seeing any meat for a week," he threatened.

She laid down, her big black head on her paws and stared at him. He hated how it unnerved him. *He* was in charge, she was his pet. His goddamn pet!

He moved to open the cage, to show her who he was. He'd take that damn collar off and she would still just sit there like a dumb lump, he knew it. He wasn't afraid.

"You down there, cuz?" Glen's voice drifted down the stairwell, stopping him.

Brandon turned from the cage. "Yeah! Coming up," he called back. A shiver of sensation ran across his back and his neck prickled with unease; he turned slowly back to the cage.

She'd moved. Without making a sound, she now stood with her face nearly touching the bars and her teeth were bared, her eyes were sharper, and they bore into him with hatred.

"Christ," he mumbled and left in a hurry, not willing to acknowledge that maybe she was smart enough to fool him. Maybe she wasn't as lost to the animal as he thought.

"How did it go?" Glen asked as he dropped a duffle bag on the counter. It clanked, and Brandon knew immediately what was in there.

"You brought the weapons?"

"Yep, these here will work great with those wooden bullets, and I even did a little work." He pulled out a rifle with a smile of satisfaction, showing Brandon where he'd used silver paint to add designs of fangs and paw prints on the handle.

"Nice work. It went well tonight, found a bloodsucker, but the stupid bitch pulled on her leash, and I got a shot off too late, hit him, but then he disappeared."

"Want me to go down there and smack her around a bit?"

Brandon was tempted to let him. She deserved it! But then he remembered how she'd looked after he'd turned his back on her and he shook his head. "Nah, I'm going to throw her some chow. She'll need her strength so we can get back out there tomorrow night. We have to keep up patrol. We're all that stands between those bloodsuckers and the citizens of Miami."

"Hell yeah!" Glen said, picking up the rifle and pretending to shoot it.

An hour later, Brandon was silent as he threw raw steak into her cage. She was back to lying down, and she didn't move for the food, but watched him with those eyes that were far too intelligent. He'd never noticed that before. Something had changed in her tonight, and he wasn't sure he liked it.

"That's the good stuff," he found himself saying as if he expected it to please her, then chastised himself for caring. He hurried back upstairs without looking behind him, but somehow, he knew she'd moved as soon as his back was turned and if he looked, she'd be up close to the cage bars again, snarling silently at him.

Katherine dreamed of Ian. She woke up with a moan as her body shuddered so hard that for a moment, she wasn't sure it had been merely a dream. She grasped the tangled bedding and looked around the room, she was alone.

"Katherine, are you alright?" His voice floated in through the closed door.

She sighed, "Yeah, just a dream." She wanted to add *unfortunately,* but she had a feeling he didn't need any ego strokes.

He pushed the door open and filled it with his body. She couldn't make out his face and she wondered what he was thinking, wondered if he knew what she'd just been envisioning. Of course that was insane, he couldn't, he wasn't a mind reader, she was pretty sure.

"Are you feeling unwell?" He walked further into the room, and she could see his face now. It was just as unreadable as it was when completely shadowed. He could be a very frustrating man to figure out. His words were caring, but his tone was flat.

She wanted to shake him, see if she could get him to crack, a little afraid of what she might find inside his controlled exterior. "I'm fine, thanks," she said and laid down, turning her back to him.

"The sun is still quite high; you should continue resting."

That got her attention. She'd slept half the day. She turned back to him, and she was sure she saw regret on his face. But why?

He watched her for a moment as if he wanted to say something, or wanted her to, but she didn't know what to say, so she just looked at him. His eyes were deep, and she wondered how much time they held. Despite his flawless skin and young, hard body, she knew he must be far older than her. His words were kind, and his manners were gentle, but he was obviously a warrior. He wore a sword and his muscles promised harm without any weapons necessary. His kiss had been searching and soft, full of passion and desire. It had left her wanting all of him. He could take anything he wanted, and yet he didn't. He confused her, such a mass of contradictions. Like every romance hero, she thought with an internal giggle.

But this was real life, not a romance novel.

Of course, that sent her mind spinning in the direction of whether or not he truly would ever want her. She was just some dumb human who'd been in the wrong place at the wrong time. He was, well, he was something amazing, something terrifying and something mythical. He was so much more than her. Yet when he'd held her to his body, she hadn't felt like it was anything less than what he wanted in that moment. She hadn't felt like she wasn't enough, and it'd been amazing. It had healed a part of her that her ex had broken.

He gave a little sigh, then turned and left without another word, shutting the door behind him. She was left wondering. She stared up at the ceiling. What if she'd invited him to join her? Was he waiting for a sign that she was too scared to give? What would Jenny do in this situation? Probably jump him and worry about consequences later.

God, she wished she could talk to her friend about all of this. She hadn't reached out to Jenny often for advice, but she needed it now. This was exactly the type of thing Jenny would love to help her with too.

Sleep was probably not going to come easily. She felt tired, but her mind spun to all the possibilities Ian presented as she stared at the ceiling. Eventually she did drift off and once again dreamed of him, this time he stood over her, watching as she touched herself, his blue eyes bored into her, his hands gripped his sword and his mouth opened revealing his fangs, which somehow turned her on even more.

Ten

IAN LAY outside the bedroom door, guarding her. He told himself it was so he would know she was safe or if she needed something, she *was* still healing after all, but he also missed her. Missed sleeping the day away with her scent in his nostrils and the sound of her breath in his ears. It had only taken two days for him to become completely addicted to her.

The sound she'd been making moments before he opened the door to check on her had been something different than he'd ever heard from her and he wasn't sure if it was wishful thinking or not, but he could have sworn he'd heard his name on her whimper.

He wanted her and was sure she wouldn't deny him if he pursued her, but he also knew she needed to heal and she wasn't without fear. It was her fear that stopped him. She was healed enough for sex if he kept it gentle. But it would have to be her idea, and he would wait, even if it killed him. He adjusted his loincloth with a frown, it might kill him.

When he heard her gasp again a while later and this time clearly moan his name, he almost lost all control. He could tell she was asleep though, had heard her breathing return to that deep steady pace of sleep a while ago. Her unconscious mind was letting

84

her give in to the fantasy of him. He knew part of that was because of her heritage. No Descendant of Atlantis was without a draw toward their vampire masters, but it didn't take away the years of servitude the Descendants had been held in. It didn't make the Descendants forget that the vampires were predators who had enslaved them.

But Katherine didn't know all that, and if he could help it, she never would. It wasn't a lie, it was just a lack of knowledge, and she didn't need to know it to survive in his world. She only needed him.

The real lie was to himself, and he knew it.

As he envisioned what she might be dreaming, his own fantasies sprang to life in his mind and he gave in. It was more than he could resist. He remembered her sweet face staring up from where she'd knelt, offering her neck like she trusted him completely. He could have taken everything from her right then. He hissed his quick release and frowned at his hand, a very unsatis-fying substitution for her warm body.

He left his post outside her door and cleaned himself up, readying for the night's work. He hated to leave her alone, but had no choice. He had to trust she'd stay inside and safe. He had to go out and stop the horrors from descending on her. He peeked at her before leaving, she was asleep, and he dared to press his lips lightly to her forehead. She made a small noise as if sighing and it tugged at his heart. She was so beautiful, so delicate, and if he played his cards right, she would willingly be all his.

"I'll return before the sun," he whispered and left the room.

As he made his way through the city, he was glad to not run across any hints of werewolf scent.

He met Beltar and the twins at the waterline where they expected Norgis and Jovi to make an appearance from wherever they were hiding.

"The werewolf is under the control of a lone and untrained Aristotle Society member and looks near starved. If I had to guess, I'd say she hasn't been out of wolf form in years."

"That could be quite dangerous," Beltar said with a frown.

"It could also be the only thing that prevents her from trying to tear us apart. He doesn't have any idea what he's doing," Ian grunted.

"You don't think he was trained?" Beltar asked.

"Not at all. But he has a better weapon than they used to," he said, rubbing his shoulder. "Wooden bullets. I don't think we need to worry about him yet. We need to take out the immediate threat of Norgis and Jovi. Has there been any sign of their emergence?"

"No, and I'm starting to worry that they headed north in search of the Descendants already," Beltar said with frustration clear in his voice.

"The Descendants have traveled this way," Samson said, appearing in the little clearing.

"Here?" Beltar asked in surprise.

"We were tracking them north, but I caught scent of them passing this way last night and so we split up. Laric has headed north under my direction, and I came back to see if I could find them before they hit the city and ran into danger."

"Shit," Beltar said, "We need to find them before Jovi does."

"No thanks, we can handle ourselves."

Ian turned, surprised to find a woman behind him holding a sword and wearing a look of deadly intent. She was tall, muscular, and had red hair pulled back in a tight ponytail. She was all deadly business in black leather pants and black shirt. She was dressed to blend into the dark and kill whatever monsters she might find. Unlike the Aristotle Society, the Descendants of Atlantis hadn't let their training slip.

"Sorcha, why are you here? This is not a safe place for your kind," Samson hissed.

"Someone's been dropping Atlantean coins in the city. We

were alerted and figured it was necessary to check out. Looks like we were right. The Prince of Atlantis doesn't come above the waterline for vacations," she sneered, and her eyes glanced over Ian with disdain. "Or is it king now?"

"I have no interest in my father's crown," Ian snarled.

"You don't need a crown to be an asshole in charge," she said back with a wicked smile. "Not a very good one though. I smell Norgis in the city. Is that why you came?"

Ian hissed at the woman and Samson snarled behind him. "Yes, we are hunting him. He'll be returned to his prison in Atlantis soon," Ian said with determination.

"Good, but that's not everything or you wouldn't have been talking about alerting us and offering protection. We don't need protection from Norgis, humans do. We need protection from your kind," she accused and dared to jam a finger at his chest.

Ian was taken aback by her brazenness. How was she not afraid of him?

"We have a standing deal. You know we aren't a danger to you," Beltar insisted.

Sorcha scoffed. "Then why are you worried about us?"

"Jovi found The Descendants' Stone," Ian said calmly. There was no use denying it, she was already here, which put her in great danger. "You need to get yourself and any others as far from the city as possible while we handle it," Ian ordered.

"That bastard. I should have hunted him years ago. My grand-mother warned me about him. He kidnapped my father and drained him trying to get information on our clan of Descendants."

"You plan to help us instead of hiding?" Prat scoffed.

"No, I plan to take the Descendant you have shacked up in your safehouse and keep her away from your dirty fangs. She deserves better. If you don't stop your brother, Ian, I will kill him, and you, and then I'll send a fucking bomb down to Atlantis and take out everyone, like my people should have done centuries ago."

"You can't have her," Ian snarled and bared his fangs at the woman.

Samson came at him from the side, it was unexpected, and Ian didn't defend himself. He was knocked to the ground, and by the time he was back on his feet, Sorcha was gone.

"What the fuck?" Ian yelled and ran as fast as he could back to the safehouse. His heart was beating wildly, his breath gasping, everything in him was screaming to stop them from taking her. The only people capable of hiding her from him, the only people capable of making her hate him.

He leaped from the ground to the fire escape, not bothering with stairs, but it was already too late. The window was open, and Katherine was gone.

"I'm going to kill him," Ian growled.

"She wasn't alone, Ian. Even if Samson hadn't intervened, they already had her," Beltar said behind him, his voice far too calm.

"Why the fuck did he intervene? I could have taken her for trade, or information!"

"Sorcha and Samson have a complicated past," Beltar explained.

"I'll find her," Ian growled. "They *can't* have her."

"No, we have to find your brother first. The Stone is too dangerous to wait. They won't harm one of their own. She's safe with them. Safer than here in the city with Jovi and Norgis," Beltar reasoned.

"Where the hell do you think Jovi and Norgis are headed, Beltar? The reason they aren't here creeping through the city this night? They got what they needed here and left. If they find the Descendants before us, *then* we'll have a problem. Then they are *all* in danger! Fuck! If I lose her—" Ian couldn't even finish that thought and an understanding settled on his friend's face.

"So let's go," Beltar hissed.

"We waste time standing around talking," Samson hissed, stepping from the shadows.

Ian glared at his friend but nodded. The man would protect Sorcha the same way he wanted to protect Katherine, he could see it burning in his eyes and he understood. "I will be honored to have you at my side, but don't get in my way again."

"I'll do what I have to," Samson said and raised his chin a notch.

Katherine was stumbling out of the bedroom with no real idea of what time it might be when they busted through the window.

A group of five armed men and women were soon standing in the room with her, and she had no idea if she should scream and run or wait and see what new insanity was about to enter her life.

"You are a Descendant," a man said after a moment of them eyeballing each other.

"A what?"

The man rolled back his sleeve and revealed a birthmark exactly like hers. "My name is Chase, and I am a Descendant of Atlantis, as are you. We are here to bring you out of the vampire's hold and to safety with us."

"Oh, um, I'm Katherine," she said dumbly as she tried to decide what the hell was going on and really wishing Ian was here.

"We must go now, Katherine. He could return at any time."

"Ian? I don't think I'm in danger from Ian."

"Trust us, you are. We will explain everything, but we must go now."

She didn't miss the way his eyes looked at her neck and she was glad Ian hadn't taken blood from there. Something told her they wouldn't look kindly on that. She resisted the urge to cover the healing red marks on her wrist.

"You've been injured," he pointed out, obviously noticing the healing skin on the front of her neck.

"I was attacked by a monster at work. Ian saved me."

Chase snorted but didn't comment.

"Why am I in danger?"

"We will explain everything once we are away. You must trust us that the vampire means you harm and slavery, no matter what he may have promised." He paused and looked mildly annoyed. "We are your family. Trust us."

After everything she'd experienced in the last few days, she was willing to believe almost anything. She looked at these people and she had to admit she felt a kinship to them, but it would take more than that for her to believe Ian meant to harm her. The possibility of insight into where she'd come from won her over, though. Whatever was going on with Ian, she could investigate further when she had all the information about her past. She had a feeling these people wouldn't be so willing to tell her anything if she was sleeping with their enemy.

"Okay," she whispered and stepped forward.

They rushed her out the window, down the fire escape, and loaded her into the back of a car. She was on her way out of the city fast, away from Ian, and not completely sure she'd made the right choice. The car came to a very sudden stop alongside the road just outside of the city and a woman wearing a lot of leather with blazing red hair and a firm look of annoyance on her face hopped in next to her.

"Drive! No doubt he followed me," she grumbled and looked over at Katherine. "You're the missing Descendant?"

"Apparently."

"And you were being held prisoner by Ian; or shacked up with him?" she asked with only curiosity and not accusation, despite the harshness of the words.

Katherine felt her face heat at the implications anyway. "Neither; he saved my life, and I was healing under his watch."

Chase huffed disbelief in the front seat, but Sorcha nodded knowingly. "Well, I'm glad you're with us now."

Katherine suddenly wasn't. She felt more like a prisoner now than she had in the apartment with Ian.

They drove the rest of the night and through the day without stopping except for gas. During that time, Katherine learned an alternate history that astounded her.

Before time was kept, vampires and monsters ruled the earth. The vampires ruled in the city of Atlantis and kept the human citizens of Atlantis as slaves, blood donors, and servants in exchange for the vampires' protection from the monsters who ruled outside the city. The vampires used a powerful Stone to make them malleable and happy without having to keep a direct hold on their thoughts. A vampire on its own could control only one mind at a time, and it would wear off after a time of being apart. The Stone acted like a spell encasing the entire city, holding the minds hostage to the influence of the vampires.

The vampire king had a favorite among the blood slave citizens. Elantra was beautiful and smart and the king gave her his blood to keep her from being influenced by any vampire or the Stone, so that she would never fall victim to the fangs or desire of another. But this allowed Elantra to think for herself, to realize that the enslavement wasn't fair, wasn't in the best interest of the Atlanteans, and so she worked out a plan. She convinced the king that in order to protect the world, the vampires must capture the monsters, imprison them within the city, and then sink the city of Atlantis to the bottom of the ocean. This way, the monsters would never again be allowed to wreak havoc on the earth and its human inhabitants outside of the city of Atlantis.

The blood slaves of Atlantis were expected to go down with the city, to offer themselves as sacrifice to the vampires in thanks for saving the human race. But during one of the celebrations, the Stone was taken, locked in a wooden box and hidden in the city. This broke the spell and allowed the human Atlanteans to escape just as the city sank and the sun rose. The vampires continued to guard the monsters and protect the human race despite what they considered a betrayal by their beloved slaves. The Descendants of those human Atlanteans had remained hidden on earth since that day, fearful that the Stone would once again be found and used to enslave them.

That time had come. Jovi, Ian's brother, had come into possession of it, it is what was found by Norgis in the museum when he attacked Katherine. This meant they were in serious danger. They would be enslaved, ordered to return to live in Atlantis, under water forever, feeding and serving the bloodthirsty vampires once again.

The picture Chase painted with his words was terrible and nothing like the man Katherine wanted to think Ian was. "Why do the vampires want us? Why not take just any human?" Katherine asked Sorcha.

"Because the Stone won't work on regular humans. Its powers draw on our blood, our heritage, and it will force us to obey their will. They bred us special, within the walls of Atlantis. Perfectly paired to react to the magic in the Stone. It was a sea witch's spell," Sorcha explained. "And it has lasted all this time."

"The birthmark," Katherine said.

"Exactly. It's the proof that the sea witch's magic still holds strong."

"So, the vampire who stole the Stone, Jovi, wants us as slaves? But the others, they aren't working with him?"

"It would seem so." Sorcha said. "Ian seems to want to stop him. I hope he does. Otherwise, we are all in trouble."

"Only if they find us," Chase said with a laugh.

"We have a very safe place," Sorcha assured her.

"Do you know who my parents were?" Katherine asked hopefully.

"We don't think your mother was a Descendant, but your father must have been one of us. Likely he didn't even know your mother conceived and so never worried about you existing out there in danger. A female Descendant never would have let a child go unprotected."

Katherine had to agree that made the most sense. "So my father could still be alive?" she asked hopefully.

"Hard to say," Sorcha said with a shrug.

Katherine wasn't sure how she felt about that possibility. She'd loved her adopted parents and had never searched out anyone else, but it would feel good to make a connection to her heritage. Of course, she was getting a big dose of that right now with these people, and she wasn't sure she was glad.

"But I'm only half then. Would it even control me?" she wondered aloud.

"If the blood in you is strong enough to produce a birthmark, then there is no doubt it will control you. You are not safe, Katherine, not unless you're behind our compound walls," Chase said fiercely.

Katherine settled in, deep in thought. She couldn't get Ian out of her mind, his gentleness, and his kiss. She'd never really felt in danger with him. But had he been lying to her, waiting for the right time to enslave her? She drifted to sleep with uncertainty in her mind.

The sun was about to set again when they arrived at a castle surrounded by a large fenced yard and beyond the castle, from what she could see, was nothing but trees. It looked like it could keep someone in as well as out, and that didn't sit well with her.

"Not only are we situated in the middle of nowhere here, but the place was spelled by a witch years ago. No one will find this place unless they are like us," Sorcha explained.

"A Descendant of Atlantis?" Katherine asked.

"Exactly," Sorcha said.

"Even if they managed to get close, they wouldn't be able to see the place. You can see it, even more proof that you are enough Descendant to be in danger from the Stone," Chase said. "Unless they get close enough to use the Stone to call us out, we are safe here."

"They can't track our scent here, so the chances of them getting that close are slim to none," Sorcha scoffed.

"No vampire has ever seen this place?" Katherine asked, with disbelief.

Sorcha's jaw set tight. "We are safe here," she said with a little too much emphasis to be true, but no one else in the car seemed to notice her slip.

"How long have you been the leader?" Katherine asked Sorcha.

"Ha! She wishes," Chase said as he parked in front of a massive staircase leading to front doors that looked big enough for a giant.

"Oh, I just assumed."

"My sister is in charge, but I back her up and no one questions my decisions," Sorcha spat, smacking Chase on the back of the head. "You'll meet Julie and everyone else. We are not a large clan, twenty Descendants in all, but we are powerful."

"Wow, so few."

Sorcha shrugged. "There was a large clan north of here, but they had a breach about ten years ago. We went to their aid, but it wasn't enough."

"Vampires found them?" Katherine asked with shock.

"Werewolves," Sorcha said darkly.

"Werewolves!" Katherine wasn't sure why the existence of werewolves surprised her, but she couldn't help the gasp of disbelief.

"So now this is all that's left, which makes it even more wonderful that we found you," Chase said, opening her door.

Katherine was nervous as she stepped out of the car and when the doors opened, and people poured out with expectant and curious faces, she wanted more than anything to be back home in her own bed.

"Welcome home," a woman said, stepping forward. She was older than Sorcha but looked similar enough with her red hair and pale skin, she had to be the sister, Julie. "And I see a new face! You found a sister for us to embrace?"

"We did. She was being held by the Atlantean prince. Ian is on land hunting his brother and Norgis," Sorcha explained.

"Hunting or joining," Chase huffed.

Katherine tried not to react to the comments but her mind whirled at the word *prince*. Ian was a prince! "I wasn't captive. He healed me."

"Yes, and you got hurt because he didn't do his job and keep Norgis in prison," Sorcha pointed out.

Katherine wasn't sure she could argue that point, so she kept silent.

Eleven

THE FIRST NIGHT they hadn't made it far from Miami before they'd had to stop for the day in the basement of an abandoned farmhouse. Samson's story had been forced out of him there. Ian had needed the reassurance that Samson could lead them in the right direction.

Samson had found Sorcha standing over the decapitated body of a naked young man in the middle of the woods. At first glance Samson had assumed that she was a witch, and this was a spell she was working. He was poised to kill her before she even noticed him there. When she reached up and slipped off her hood he saw it, the mark of the Descendants of Atlantis was there on the back of her neck.

She was no witch. Whatever happened from there, Ian couldn't get Samson to clarify, beyond the fact that they spent a significant amount of time together before he dropped her off at their compound.

Ian had been reassured that night when the fierceness and speed with which Samson ran across the land had matched his own need to get to the compound. They'd run into Laric, who was crisscrossing the area in hopes of finding a weakness in their spell to indicate where the compound stood. He hadn't had any luck yet and Samson said it was a bit farther north, but time was too short. They couldn't risk trying to break in and have the sun rise. They needed a full night to descend upon the compound and enter before the Descendants had a chance to run off and hide again.

So here they were, in the basement of a farmhouse, irritated with each other and waiting for the damn sun to set.

"I won't be able to pinpoint the location exactly. Their spells are too good, but I remember some landmarks. We'll get close. If Jovi and Norgis are in the area, if they plan what we think they plan, then we'll be right there to intervene," Samson explained for the thousandth time.

Ian knew everyone was getting annoyed with his worrying, but they didn't understand. His connection to her was consuming. If he didn't find her, if he wasn't able to save her from whatever Jovi planned, he would burn the world down around those who had stood in his way, friends or not. He glanced at Samson's stoic face and saw a determination that mirrored his own and a pain that could only come from separation from one's mate. Perhaps he understood.

"Why do you think he chose Norgis?" Ian said, thinking aloud.

Beltar looked thoughtful. "Jovi is a smart man. He chose the dumbest of monsters to assist him. I don't think that was an accident."

Ian knew Beltar was right. There were monsters locked away in Atlantis that could do horrifying things. The fact that he chose to free a monster who was no better than a mindless slave himself was interesting. "What benefit is Norgis?" Ian mumbled.

Katherine woke up and the sun was high in the sky. She'd slept long and hard and if she weren't in a strange room, she would have thought everything had been a very vivid bad dream. But here she was in a castle with, supposedly, some relatives of sorts, and they were all hiding away from vampires. She shook her head and sat up wondering what the hell she was supposed to do now. She had no desire to stay here and hide for the rest of her life. She also didn't want to be anyone's blood slave. Julie definitely seemed to think those were the only two options for any of them.

Katherine was pretty certain she'd made the wrong choice back in that Miami apartment. She never should have left without at least talking to Ian first. But after getting here, she wondered if they would have given her any option if she hadn't gone willingly. Unsure what else to do, she got up and showered. She found a pile of clean clothes on the bed when she left the bathroom, pulled them on gratefully, then headed out to face her captors, because that's what they were, she had to admit. Armed guards stood at the doors and fence; this wasn't a place she could just leave. Images of Ian's face kept popping into her mind. She wondered if he knew where she'd gone, if he cared or worried. Did he think she'd run away? He'd told her she could leave any time, he wouldn't have stopped her, and that had made her feel safe. She remembered his touches, his heated looks, and the way he'd said he would fuck her in the kitchen. Her body heated, and she wanted so badly to go back in time and tell him to go ahead and do it. She was afraid now it was too late; she'd probably never get the chance to experience him, and that thought was depressing as hell.

And so was all this.

She'd gotten a little more information before begging for a bed the night before. These people were basically self-sufficient and only left when absolutely necessary and always during the day, fully armed. Behind the main house was a large garden and greenhouse and orchard with fresh fruit. They had livestock as well; she could hear cows and pigs from her room. It was a fine place, she supposed, especially if you had grown up with these people and were afraid of living out in the open where vampires or werewolves might find you.

She was definitely afraid of werewolves.

Katherine made her way downstairs and ran into Sorcha stomping from an open doorway. When she got close, she saw it was an office and Julie sat behind a desk looking regal. Bookshelves lined the walls, one filled with books that looked old enough to interest her. Most had no title on the bindings but, she saw one that said Vampires and another Atlantis and she wondered if these would hold the history of all of them.

Chase was standing near Julie with a large smile on his face and doe eyes as he gazed at Julie, who had a book open on the desk in front of her. She slammed it closed as Katherine approached.

"Katherine! Just the girl we wanted to see," Chase called out when he noticed her.

"I guess I slept in," she said awkwardly as she entered the room.

"Tell me more about why you were shacked up with the Prince," Julie said with a frown.

Prince, Katherine had almost forgot about that piece. It didn't fit Ian. He wasn't regal or entitled. He was a warrior, if anything. She couldn't imagine him sitting on a throne, or even behind a desk like this and lording his power over others. Julie certainly seemed to enjoy the position, however.

Katherine couldn't help feeling defensive at the loaded question. She crossed her arms and raised an eyebrow; she didn't intimidate that easily. "Well, I had just woken up in a strange house with a strange man, if that's what you mean." She hadn't been doing anything wrong, and not only that, but Ian had saved her life. She had no doubt.

"The vampires would like nothing more than to enslave our kind once again," Julie said angrily.

"He saved my life," Katherine snapped back, not willing to let this woman tell her Ian had ulterior motives. "I was torn apart by some kind of monster!"

"Yes, a monster that he let out. Their one job was to keep those things locked away in Atlantis, and they couldn't even do that right," Julie huffed. "They don't care about humans, just what runs through our veins."

Katherine took a breath and assessed the situation. Julie had a very determined look on her face and she was in charge here. She obviously held a deep hate for the vampires, possibly for good reason. Sorcha didn't seem to feel quite as strongly about the vampires, more cautious than outright hateful, but definitely didn't like the werewolves. It didn't leave Katherine with a very firm idea of where her own feelings should lie. She knew she didn't want to get on Julie's bad side at this point, though. Instead of incriminating herself further with this woman, she waited for Julie to make the next move, saying nothing.

"Do you think they will come for you?" Chase asked as if he couldn't care less about the answer, but Katherine would bet he cared a lot and so did Julie.

"They have the Stone. Aren't they coming for all of us?" Katherine countered, trying to see what was really going on here.

"Jovi?" Julie said with a wave of her hand. "He and the Stone are a problem for sure, but I am more curious at the moment about Ian, the Prince of Atlantis. Is *he* coming for *you*?" Her eyes were intense as she waited for Katherine to answer.

Katherine knew this woman was dangerous, could feel hatred rolling off of her and for some reason, it was very much directed at her. "I don't know why he would." She tried to make her voice flat. She would give nothing away if she could help it. But images of his passionate kiss leapt to the front of her brain and that one word, *mine*. "He did ask me to stay put in the apartment while he was gone, but I don't see any reason for him to chase me down. It wasn't an order, just a request to keep me safe while I still healed. I

THE VAMPIRES OF ATLANTIS

wasn't locked behind a wall," she said with a bit of annoyance. She was more a prisoner here than she'd been there.

"Did you let him feed from you? Do you realize that a Descendant's blood is particularly attractive to vampires?" Julie's words dripped with disgust and she twisted her lips. "You aren't special to him; he'd take Chase's blood with just as much pleasure."

"No!" Katherine gasped, hoping Julie would buy the lie. "No, I didn't know, and no, I didn't, fuck, what the hell is wrong with you?" Her body shivered with the memory of the way his fangs had slid into her skin and his soft, hot lips had caressed her wrist. She hoped Julie bought it as a shiver of disgust. "I woke up after almost dying and the man who kept me from dying was there. Then he had to leave to get supplies and your stud there busted in."

Julie ignored the stud remark, but Chase beamed as if pleased with the assessment.

"My sister thinks that Jovi is the only real danger and that we should *trust* the others. What do you think?"

This was a tricky question. Katherine could see it painted on the wall and it irked her that Julie thought she was dumb enough to fall for it. If she said she agreed and trusted even Ian, then Julie would surely think she was lost to some kind of vampire blood craze. "I don't know the others. I only met Ian and briefly at that. I can say he didn't harm me; I can't say what he would have done had I remained in the house." It wasn't a lie and Katherine spoke with confidence.

Julie nodded, seeming to accept that answer. "My scouts tell me they're bedded down for the day close by. They'll be trying to find us tonight. They won't, without help." Julie added that last with narrowed eyes, the warning clear in the way Chase touched the gun at his side.

"Then I guess they won't find us," Katherine said with a shrug. "I think I need to find some food; can you point me toward the kitchen?" she asked, hoping she didn't sound too desperate to get away from this conversation.

Julie pursed her lips as if she wanted to deny the request. "Yes, of course. Chase will show you."

"No, I can find it if you just tell me which hall to take."

Julie didn't look like she trusted Katherine one bit, and Katherine wondered if she'd made a mistake somewhere in that conversation. Where would she go if these people kicked her out? Or worse, decided she needed to be kept prisoner in a locked room, or dead! She suddenly felt very vulnerable and alone. No one would come looking for her. They already thought she was dead and dumped in a swamp to be alligator food. But Julie said Ian was near. Her body heated at that thought. He *was* coming for her.

Or was he meeting up with Jovi to use the stone against them all?

No, she dismissed the thought as soon as it came to her. She knew that Ian was not that kind of monster.

"Nonsense, you don't need to wander lost. Chase, take her to the kitchen." Julie waved a hand and Chase hopped to obey.

Katherine stood and gave Julie a tight smile. "Thanks."

"Of course, I'm here to take care of everyone."

Katherine followed Chase to the kitchen at the back of the first floor. Out the window she could see a large portion of the side yard surrounded by a high wall, and beyond that, trees.

"Thanks, I'm sure I can rummage some breakfast, or lunch I guess," she said in a dismissing tone.

Chase watched her with a distrustful look for a few minutes as she searched the fridge but left when she pulled out sandwich supplies. Katherine breathed a sigh of relief as she was left alone and just stared at the food for a minute, not really seeing it.

"What the hell have I gotten into?" she whispered.

"I need your help," Sorcha said as she rushed into the kitchen. Her eyes were wide, and her cheeks were red, like she was about to explode with whatever was on her mind.

"What could I possibly help you with?"

"You have his blood in you?"

"Oh!" Katherine's stomach threatened to unload at the memory of the last time she'd thought too hard about that fact. "Yeah, I guess I do. He was saving my life," she defended.

"Yes, I know how it works," Sorcha sighed. "We need to find them."

"Why? Aren't they coming here?" Katherine was sure this was a trick of some sort. Her eyes darted around, expecting to see Chase lurking in the doorway.

"Which is exactly why we need to find them first. Julie has called in the wolves. They'll track, and attack, and they won't leave survivors." A deep pain passed over Sorcha's face, but was quickly gone, replaced by hard determination.

"Woah, wait a minute. You want to *help* the vampires?" Katherine tried to give her best shocked and disgusted expression. If this was a trick to scout out her loyalties, she wasn't dumb enough to fall for it.

Sorcha rolled her eyes and put her hands on her hips. "Look, either help me or just shut up about it, okay? I need to warn Samson and I *thought* you'd want to warn Ian. Maybe I misjudged."

Then Katherine understood. Sorcha had feelings for the vamp named Samson, and Julie obviously wasn't a supportive sister.

"Why is she sending the wolves to kill them? They can't find us, right?"

Sorcha shrugged. "She wants more than just to hide here. She wants them gone and if they won't go back to Atlantis, she wants them dead. If she's calling in the wolf pack, then she is serious and I just—" Sorcha stopped, her voice hitched, and she took a shuddering breath. "You have no idea what kind of monsters the wolves are, Katherine." Sorcha shook her head. "Samson helped me once; I owe him this. We have to find them first and warn them."

Katherine wasn't sure she wanted to get involved with the poli-

tics at play here, but she knew she didn't believe in harming inno-
cents, and she didn't think Ian and whoever he was with meant to
harm them.

"How can I help?"

"First, we need to get out of here unnoticed."

Katherine put away the sandwich supplies she'd gotten out and
followed Sorcha into the yard.

"Most everyone else is with Julie right now getting briefed on
the situation, so we should be able to go out unnoticed, but not
through the front obviously."

Katherine expected to find a door along the wall somewhere,
but Sorcha slipped to her belly behind a row of hedges and pushed
aside a few branches to reveal a very small hole dug under a crum-
bling bit of the stone wall. Now she really felt like a prisoner.

"How long till they know we're gone?" Katherine wondered
aloud.

"Hopefully we get a couple hours. Once through the wall, we
run."

"In what direction?"

"South, as far as I can tell, that's why I need you. The call of his
blood in your veins should be strong enough to direct us more
certainly, at least until we get closer. You just have to listen in and
follow where it tells you to go."

"Fuck," Katherine grumbled as she watched Sorcha's feet
disappear under the wall. She had no idea what Sorcha was talking
about. She didn't feel any kind of call from Ian's blood.

"Come on," Sorcha hissed through the wall.

"Coming," Katherine grumbled as she slid on her belly and
ignored anything that might be moving around her. She was not a
fan of creepy crawlies.

"Run," Sorcha demanded, grabbing her arm before she was
even fully upright.

And she did. She ran and ran. Sorcha's desperation infected
her, and she ran faster than she'd ever run in her life. Through the

trees, they bolted, dodging branches, and slowing only when necessary to catch a quick breath and then run more. She really regretted not having eaten anything before following Sorcha, but she didn't stop, she didn't complain, she felt like the hounds of hell were at her heels and they weren't after her, they were after Ian and somehow that was more motivating.

After a while, she wasn't following, she was leading, and something told her she was heading in the right direction. She was being pulled toward the one who had taken her blood and who had given her his. As they got closer, she found extra strength to push faster. She knew that the only way to settle the intense feelings flowing through her would be to reach him.

Twelve

IAN COULDN'T BELIEVE he'd actually been able to doze off, but when he woke up to the sudden reality that she was close, he was thrown into a frenzy of pacing and hissing.

"What the hell, Ian?" Beltar asked as he was startled awake.

"She's coming," he snapped. "I can feel her getting closer by the second. She's searching for me, using my blood to find us."

"But why, and how the hell does she know to do that?" Beltar questioned.

"Someone must be helping her. Maybe she's in danger," he hissed, cursing the sun that still shone far too bright to risk.

"Or someone's using her to find us and kill us while the sun's up," Prat said sleepily.

"Sorcha knows," Samson said confidently. "She's helping. I can sense her nearing as well."

"What if they are bringing the whole damn clan to attack us?" Beltar hissed with sudden concern.

"No, it feels—" Ian stopped, not wanting to share the intimate things that were happening in his body at the moment. He met Samson's gaze momentarily and knew he was experiencing something similar. The knowledge that she was getting closer paired with the draw of his blood rushing through her veins. He was on edge for a lot of reasons, not all of them appropriate to share with his men. "It feels like desperation and fear. If she was coming to attack, it would be anger and betrayal," he finally said as explanation and Samson nodded agreement.

"You think she fell in love with you in a day and now seeks you out in the middle of nowhere, away from certain safety behind stone walls," Prat said with a laugh. "And how was the lady's—" his words were cut off by Samson's fist and it was the only thing that saved him from Ian tearing him apart.

"I don't know why she's coming; I just know she is, and quickly," he gritted out.

They all waited silently, no one sure what to expect when the women arrived.

Katherine knew they were close. She could feel the tingling in her veins increase, driving her to turn and head off through a thicket of trees then veer left and head straight toward a hill. "I think it's just on the other side of that," she gasped, barely able to keep breathing with the pace she was still going. They had slowed a bit, but they hadn't stopped, both determined to beat the beasts and the sunset.

When they crested the hill, an abandoned farmhouse came into view. "They must be in there, probably has a root cellar where they can hide from the sun," Sorcha panted.

And that's when it hit her. She was running *toward* vampires, away from humans that she was supposedly related to, and the possibility of *werewolves!* "What the fuck am I doing?" she whispered.

"You're saving lives, trust me," Sorcha said, giving her a push down the hill.

She definitely didn't fully trust Sorcha, but she knew Julie was dangerous and, most importantly, she knew Ian wasn't, so she continued on.

The front door was missing, and they panted as they peered into what looked mostly like rotten wood and dirt.

"Hello!" Katherine called. "We are here with some information," she added, hoping they wouldn't be quick to attack. Ian wasn't the only vampire here apparently.

"We're in the basement," Ian shouted.

Sorcha pushed ahead, unafraid, and Katherine followed, nervous. But when they descended an old staircase into a damp dark cellar and Ian stood looking at her with an intensity that took her breath away, she felt safe, and she felt right.

"Katherine," he said with a hiss as he crossed the room and grabbed her shoulders. "Are you okay?"

"Yes, but you guys may not be," she said with a shaky smile.

"Sorcha," a large, angry-looking vampire whispered harshly, taking a step toward Sorcha, but freezing at the frown on her face.

"Don't touch me, Samson," Sorcha snapped, even though he was still half a room away.

Katherine eyed the vampire warily; this was the one that Sorcha knew. Obviously, something had gone sour in their relationship.

"What did you come to tell us? How did you escape?" Ian prodded, drawing her attention back to him.

"My sister called in the wolves," Katherine panted, trying to keep her eyes locked on Ian and ignore the fact that there were five other men in a very small dark space with her. The one that was staring at Sorcha like he wanted to devour her was huge, maybe even bigger than Ian. He had short black hair, and his eyes were an amazing purple color that she envied. Near the back stood a man with a relaxed smile and long blond hair. His green eyes were friendly, and Katherine immediately felt she could trust this one. Next to him stood two who looked similar enough to be twins, both with brown hair, one's long and one's short. They were looking at her like she was a snack, and she couldn't help taking a small step back. Noticing this reaction, the last one, a blond, mohawk'd man with assessing blue eyes, gave them both a sharp hiss. A warning? They were all attractive, all pale, and deadly looking. These were vampires. She was in a room with six vampires. Her heart hammered in her chest.

Ian's hand gripped her shoulder, and his intense gaze wasn't helping her feel relaxed. "They won't harm you," he said with a calm that didn't match his intensity.

Katherine met his gaze, and she gave a shaky smile. "I don't know what I'm doing," she admitted.

He smiled back at her and the twins in the back of the room made kissy noises that were so uncanny coming from vampires, she was shaken out of her fear. Ian made quick introductions then. No one moved to shake her hand, and she was thankful for that.

"What the hell is Julie doing, working with the wolves?" Samson snarled when the pleasantries were done. He closed the distance between himself and Sorcha then, despite her snarl to stay back.

"She's lost it," Sorcha gritted out. "And I don't know if the others will realize it before it's too late."

Samson looked like he was ready to kill, and Katherine took a step back.

"Calm yourself," Ian commanded. "We have to prepare for battle."

"No, you need to leave!" Sorcha said, and Katherine nodded her head in agreement.

"The sun is up," Beltar said in a sardonic tone. This was the leader of the coven that lived above the waterline, Ian had told her, and she could see why. He was calm and controlled, but something in his voice demanded obedience. Even she snapped to attention when he spoke.

"I know," Sorcha hissed, obviously unafraid of the vampire leader. "Sunset will be too late."

"You two should leave," Ian said, his eyes intense on Katherine. "Get away before the wolves are here."

"No, they should stay," Beltar said, surprising everyone. "Jovi and Norgis are still out there, and close, no doubt. If Jovi catches them after sunset..." He didn't need to finish that sentence and a spiral of fear started to twist in her stomach.

Katherine had almost forgotten about that threat looming over her. How had her life become so complicated? "We still get to risk being taken under Jovi's weird mind control?" Katherine guffawed. "Maybe we *should* run!"

"Actually, neither of you are at risk of that," Samson said with a look that didn't completely hide his discomfort.

"What are you talking about?" Sorcha demanded.

"The stone doesn't work on you if you've had vamp blood recently, you've both had it to heal from near fatal wounds in the last year. He won't be able to control you."

Katherine's eyes darted to Ian with shock.

"So what's the plan?" Sorcha gritted out.

Beltar took a deep breath and the other vampires in the room stepped forward, looking eager. "We fight."

When the sun went down, they were on the move, up and out of the cellar. They'd come up with a plan, and she hoped they would survive. She wasn't sure what her life was going to be like after this, but whatever it was, it would be better than the way it would have ended on the floor of the museum storage, surrounded by broken artifacts.

They didn't make it far from the farmhouse before a rotten smell filled her with terror. She couldn't stop herself from grabbing onto Ian's arm as the group stopped in a small clearing. They'd been heading toward the Descendants' compound, having decided to face the threat head on and offer an alliance against Jovi.

"Norgis," Beltar hissed.

Ian shoved Katherine behind him, and she didn't even complain, she didn't want to face that monster again.

"Brother," a smooth voice said from behind.

The entire group spun around at the word, and there, at the edge of the woods, stood a dark version of Ian. Katherine's eyes devoured the sight of him. Tall and muscled, black hair piled into a bun on top of his head, dark stubble on his chin and eyes that nearly glowed they were such a bright green. Behind him stood the beast, and Katherine shuddered. Its red eyes glowed out of a black face that wept with something that smelled like death and decay. Bile rose in her throat, but she swallowed it back, barely. Long flaming red hair hung loose around his bare form and his red eyes looked at her with recognition. She knew that his teeth were sharp as razors and on his hands, claws thick and long, could cut through her like she was nothing. She was frozen in fear as she stared into the face of the thing that had nearly killed her.

"Jovi, you have gone against everything we stand for," Ian accused, thankfully drawing Katherine out of her fearful thoughts. She clung to him; she was safe because of him.

"No," Jovi sneered. "I rejected what Father made us become, what he changed us into. Do you even remember what it used to be like? The way we were worshipped and served by beautiful blood bags," he smiled wickedly, his eyes landing on Katherine. "I see you do remember that part, at least."

Ian hissed and pulled out his sword. "You don't have any idea what I am about, Brother."

Jovi held up a gold chain and from it hung a green stone, bright in the moonlight. Katherine gasped, recognizing the stone she'd seen in the small broken box before Norgis had attacked.

"Come to me, little ones," he whispered.

Katherine felt the words caress her mind and tug at her, but she didn't move. Beside her, she felt Sorcha stiffen and Katherine wondered if it was harder for her, because Samson's blood wasn't as fresh in her body. She would willingly drink Ian's blood every day to keep herself from becoming a slave to Jovi.

Jovi frowned. "I said, come here, slaves!" he said with a little more force this time.

Norgis made a gurgling growl sound that sent a chill down Katherine's spine.

"You're too late. We've claimed them," Samson said darkly. "Elevated them from slaves to wives. You cannot control them."

Sorcha made a strangled sound of shock and Katherine whipped her head around to glare at Ian. "Excuse me?" Katherine said with a poke to his shoulder for emphasis.

Ian ignored her. "You can't take us all on, not even with that thing at your side," he motioned to Norgis. "And do you smell that? The wolves have been sicced on all of us. You'd better run, brother," Ian said darkly. "If the wolves don't tear you apart, I will."

"Your monster can't save you from the wolves," Beltar added.

"You haven't stopped me," Jovi said, "and neither will a pack of dogs." Then he disappeared in a flash of movement, Norgis moving behind him with surprising quickness.

"Explain!" Katherine said when they were gone.

"No time, they're almost upon us," Ian said. "Remember the plan."

Katherine wanted to argue but she could hear noises now, the snap of a twig and the growl of a wolf. It was no time to argue about verbiage.

Sorcha grabbed Katherine's arm, and they scrambled into position. They were to wait high in a tree and basically watch the battle without distracting the men. The vampires were confident they would win, as long as they didn't have to waste any energy worrying about delicate humans; or so Prat had said, not so delicately, earning hisses from both Ian and Samson.

Katherine watched in horror as shadows moved and a dozen giant wolves emerged with snarling faces and bared fangs. The vampires were outnumbered and surrounded. The tight set to Ian's jaw told her he hadn't expected this. There were a lot of wolves.

"What's going to happen?" Katherine whispered to Sorcha.

"I don't know," Sorcha said with a trembling voice. Her eyes were locked onto the line of wolves and her face had gone so pale that Katherine thought she must be about to pass out.

"Sorcha?" Katherine whispered. "Are you okay?"

Then a growl rippled through the pack and Katherine could think of nothing other than what she was witnessing below. All six vampires were standing ready, swords drawn. The pack closed in around them and then everyone was moving at such a pace it was almost a blur to watch. Thuds and grunts were followed by shouts and growls. Every once in a while, something flew into a nearby tree and stood still long enough for her to assess damage. Sometimes it was a wolf, sometimes it was a vampire, and neither stayed down for long.

"They're going to kill each other," Katherine whispered, wondering how this could possibly end without everyone bleeding profusely.

"If we're lucky," Sorcha whispered back.

Katherine was about to pinch the woman and make her admit she didn't want Samson to be killed when a gunshot cut through the air, followed by another and another. Katherine screamed as hands grabbed her and forced her to the ground at the feet of three very large, very naked men.

"Ian!" she screamed, but heard nothing in response. It was over, and they'd lost. No one had said to expect guns.

"What the hell kind of guns were those?" Sorcha demanded as she was thrown down at Katherine's side.

The large men leered down at them, their faces were swollen and there were cuts on their chests. They hadn't gotten through the fight unscathed; that knowledge was little comfort when she had no idea if Ian was still alive. She didn't even want to think about what was about to become of herself. If Sorcha's reaction was any indication, this was the worst-case scenario.

"Splinter bullets," one man said with a laugh. "Even better than the wooden ones, these break apart on impact and it's nearly impossible to remove all the pieces. Your vampire friends are going to die. You're welcome." The other two laughed in agreement.

"Fuck you," Sorcha spat and stood defiantly, hands on hips and glaring.

Katherine followed suit, but she didn't have the energy or confidence to curse at their captors. The best she could do was offer support by standing beside Sorcha and trying not to cry as the adrenaline started to fade and reality became all too concerning.

"What do you think? You can just kill them and take us? Didn't work well last time one of you tried that with me," Sorcha spat at the one who had spoken. "I'll cut your head off the first chance I get."

The man's eyes flashed yellow, and a growl rumbled his chest. "You'd never get the chance with me."

"Manhandle me again and we'll see," Sorcha snapped.

The man slapped her so hard she stumbled and probably would have fallen if Katherine hadn't caught her. The other two looked on with jeering smiles and bared teeth. Katherine didn't like how much they seemed to enjoy the violence.

"I don't know what's going on but—" Katherine began, hoping she could talk her way out of this.

"Shut up," the man snapped and grabbed her chin in a tight grip. "I have no use for vampire whores, but I promised not to kill you two."

"Yet," one of the others added with a laugh.

Katherine looked at Sorcha for answers, but she was just glaring ahead, her breath coming in pants and looking like she was going to explode.

"Tie them up," the man commanded to his two comrades,

then he turned around and his body shifted smoothly into the form of a large black wolf. Katherine wondered if that was the leader. Their chances were looking less and less promising by the second.

Their hands were bound, and they were marched by naked men that were bruised and bleeding but didn't seem to be slowed by it in the least. She caught sight of a few dead, or at least seriously wounded, being taken along as well. She was uncomfortable with the feeling of vindication that gave her. Their vampires were unconscious and being carried. All of them had wounds from the fight and all of them were bleeding profusely from their chests. The bullets were working too well. Fear and anger filled Katherine. She so badly wanted to rush over to Ian, to save him, but there was nothing she could do.

"Why are they unconscious?" Katherine whispered to Sorcha.

"The splinter bullets, they shot them right over the heart. If their bodies aren't able to expel every splinter fast enough, it's going to kill them."

Tears stung the backs of Katherine's eyes and she let her mind focus on the fear of what might happen to Ian, ignoring the fact that she was currently tied up and being marched into uncertainty and possible torture, or death, herself. She wanted to ask Sorcha so many questions, but she didn't dare, not with so many ears so close, so many supernatural ears. Her eyes stayed on Ian's limp form; it took two massive men to carry him. *Wake up!* She willed, hoping there was something to their blood bond that would get through to him.

She couldn't explain it, but the grief over his situation was deep and overruled her personal concern. She could only assume it had to do with his blood in her system. "Let me check on him," she demanded to no one in particular. Any of the human shaped werewolves could help her.

None responded.

"I said let me go to him! If you don't intend to kill him, then let me go to him!"

"Who said we don't intend to kill him?" one of the men said with a laugh.

Katherine's stomach clenched. Sorcha's eyes were locked onto Samson's body. Whatever was going on between them hurt Sorcha just as much as Ian's limp body was hurting Katherine. She wished she could hug the woman, wished they could come together and comfort each other, but she knew Sorcha wouldn't welcome it and it would only show more weakness to their captors. So she mourned alone as they walked.

"Patrick, you have returned, my sister! I am so glad she's safe." Julie's eyes narrowed on Sorcha as they approached the walls of the compound. Julie was standing just inside the gate with her arms crossed and her feet apart. No hint of fear at the approaching wolf pack or its prisoners.

"How could you?" Sorcha hissed and spat at her sister.

Julie wiped the spittle off her shoulder and glared. "How could I? You warned them. You chose vampires against your own kind, sister. What would Father have said?" Julie accused.

"You know what *they* are," Sorcha hissed and jutted her chin toward the wolf man beside her. "And it's so much worse. Samson saved my life after one of them nearly took it," she whispered.

"At what cost?" Julie said stiffly. "Take them all into the dungeon."

"Bitch!" Sorcha screamed as the wolves continued into the house.

Katherine couldn't speak as they were dragged down the stairs and thrown into a holding cell. She wanted to scream at the men as they dropped Ian carelessly onto the hard floor.

"Good luck with that," the apparent leader, Patrick, said with a snarl. "If they manage to wake up before they die, they'll be in such a frenzy they'll rip your throats out as their last undead act. Nothing less than vampire whores deserve, though."

Thirteen

As soon as they were alone, Katherine threw herself across the cell and onto the ground next to Ian. There was so much blood, it was oozing from his chest wound and the scratches and cuts over the rest of his body looked like they were as fresh as ever.

"They should be healing," Sorcha said, and Katherine realized she too was crouched on the ground staring down at a wounded vampire, Samson.

"What do we do?"

"Untie me." Sorcha turned and bent forward, pushing her bound wrists out.

"How the hell am I supposed to do that?"

"Use your fucking teeth for all I care. Just get it done!"

Katherine stared down at the knotted rope around Sorcha's wrists and bit her lip. This wasn't going to work. Then she remembered a glint of steel as they'd been shoved across the yard toward the house. She scrambled over Ian's dying body to Laric. She backed into his body and patted around his midsection, accidentally slapping a hand against his dick, but it was worth it, she felt a prick on her finger. He had a small dagger.

It wasn't easy, but with backs together, Katherine managed to cut through Sorcha's ropes and free her hands. It was moments later that Katherine's hands were free. She stared at Sorcha, wide eyed and terrified. "What now?"

"We have to get the splinters out, *all* of them."

"How?" Katherine eyed the dagger in Sorcha's hand, visualizing cutting into Ian's flesh to pick out splinters of wood. Her stomach twisted.

Sorcha must have noticed where Katherine's gaze was because she dropped the knife and huffed. "The knife would be too slow; we have to suck them out."

Katherine did a slow blink. "Excuse me?" Bile rose in her throat; she'd rather slice and dice him like a roast chicken.

Sorcha didn't hesitate though. She bent over Samson's chest and started to suck. It wasn't long until she lifted her head and spit a spray of blood out. A closer look revealed it was littered with wooden splinters. It was working!

"Fuck," Katherine groaned as she turned to Ian. She knew she had to do it; knew she would do whatever necessary to save him. "You better get us out of here," she whispered as she leaned forward. Something told her she didn't want to die with his blood coursing through her veins.

She leaned down and pressed her open mouth to the worst of the wounds. It was directly over his heart. His blood hit her tongue, and she had to force back a gag as the warm liquid quickly filled her senses. She pushed away the thoughts of what it was and just did it. She sucked hard, and almost pulled away when a sharp splinter hit her tongue, but it told her it was working so she sucked again, filling her mouth and trying hard not to swallow. She pulled away, turned her head and spit, then dipped back down and did it again. Over and over until she no longer felt the sting of splinters and the taste no longer triggered her gag reflex. She could admit it held a musty sweetness, and the smell reminded her of life, something she wanted them both to keep experiencing.

She pulled back, mouth dripping, and looked down at his face. He'd made a sound, a small groan. He was waking up!

"Katherine?" he whispered, eyes fluttering.

"Yeah, could you do me a favor and not die? I think you're my only chance of survival here," she said with a laugh that sounded more than a little erratic.

"What the fuck?" he groaned as he sat up. His hand came up to her face, wiping away blood. "Is this yours or mine?"

"Yours, I-I had to," she said. Her voice hitched, and tears stung her eyes.

He smiled a crooked half smile, his eyes closing halfway as they stared at her mouth. "You sucked a lot of blood, love. You have no idea what you're in for."

"I'm not your wife," she said quickly, remembering what he'd said to Jovi.

He just laughed and leaned forward to give her a quick, but surprisingly deep, kiss. "You're my everything," he whispered. "But what matters now is my men. I must help them."

As Ian and Samson moved to help the others, sucking the splinters out in half the time it had taken Katherine and Sorcha, Katherine's mind swam, her body warmed, and she was pretty sure the blood was acting like an aphrodisiac by the way her nipples tightened, and her thighs tingled. It was embarrassing when she accidentally let a quiet moan slip, but a quick glance told her Sorcha was in a similar state.

When the others were awake and recovering, Sorcha relayed what had occurred after they'd been shot and passed out. Ian joined Katherine where she sat and pulled her against his body, holding her close possessively. She didn't try to move away. She wanted to stay wrapped in the safety of his arms forever.

"I'm sorry," he whispered in her ear, so quiet she wasn't sure she heard it at first. His hands rubbed her arms gently, and it sent tingles straight to her core. She had a feeling he knew it, too, because the smile he gave her when she tilted her head was wicked.

"For what, exactly?"

"For not being able to properly soothe the ache I know you're feeling after taking all of that blood from me."

She looked away to hide her own smile. Yeah, he knew.

Sorcha finished her explanation and the vampires in the room looked ready to murder someone.

"Fuck," Beltar said as he rubbed his already healing chest wound. "What did the wolves offer your sister?" he asked Sorcha.

"I'm afraid nothing. I think she's just gotten her mind so twisted she can't see they are a bigger threat."

"Is there a way out of here?" Samson asked.

"No, this place was designed for this. There's only one entrance, no doubt heavily guarded. If they shoot you guys again, they won't give us a chance to remove the splinters," Sorcha said darkly.

"They want us dead, but they also could have left us in the clearing. So they want something else too," Samson reasoned.

"Do you think they expected us to save you?" Katherine asked with disbelief.

"There's more than one cage down here," Ian pointed out. "If they hadn't put us all in one, you wouldn't have been able to do anything except watch us die."

"So they wanted us to save you, why?" Sorcha wondered aloud.

"I think we're about to find out," Beltar said as the door at the top of the stairs opened.

Patrick walked down. He was wearing a pair of jeans now, still no shirt or shoes and he had a wide grin on his face. The smell of dog assaulted Katherine's nostrils, and she gagged, plugging her nose. "What the hell?" she whispered.

"The vamp blood is going to mess with your senses for a bit," Sorcha explained.

"Well, well, well, looks like you ladies are just as great at sucking as I would have expected of a couple vamp whores."

Katherine rolled her eyes at the insult and Sorcha snorted, but Ian and Samson hissed, taking offense for them. They were pushed to the back of the cell behind all of the vamps and Katherine couldn't help feeling a squeeze of pleasure at such protectiveness.

"What do you want?" Ian demanded.

"I want the assistance of one of the top curators of the museum in Miami, actually," Patrick said, grinning wide and showing off his large inhuman teeth.

Katherine gasped and Ian hissed.

"Go eat a sliver bullet. She's not helping you with shit," Sorcha snapped.

"Well then, all her lovely friends will die. It seems this basement is fitted with quite the contraption, a skylight of sorts. It is really just a relay of mirrors that bring in light from above when activated, but I hear it's strong enough to kill a vampire." His eyes turned yellow as he spoke, relishing the thought of destroying the vampires he'd captured.

The thought sickened Katherine. She didn't know these men well, but she had no doubt that they weren't monsters who deserved to die in the sun, and without Sorcha snapping a denial of such a possibility, she was helpless to do anything but agree.

"What do you need?" she gritted out, pushing her way to the front of the group. Ian looked at her with a scowl of disapproval.

"That's a good girl. I'll tell you on the way to the city," Patrick said.

Katherine took a step back. "I won't be going anywhere with you alone."

"I don't think you have much choice. I hold all the cards, my dear."

Katherine cursed under her breath and Ian's chest rumbled with anger. All around her, she heard hisses of disagreement.

"You won't harm *any* of them," she demanded.

"They will be unharmed by the wolves," Patrick agreed.

"And freed?" she said, feeling more confident.

"Well now, that's more of a Julie negotiation. After all, I did promise her I'd deliver her sister and the vampires in exchange for the Descendant who can access what I need." He grinned, knowing he had them all by the balls.

Katherine wanted to argue, wanted to negotiate, wanted there to be something they could threaten this idiot with, but when she looked at Sorcha for help, she just shrugged. Ian wouldn't look at her. He was glaring daggers at Patrick and baring his fangs. The other vampires all had blank faces as they looked at her, waiting for her answer. She had a feeling if she refused, they'd be okay with that, even if it was signing their death warrants. They wouldn't willingly put her into harm, and that solidified her resolve. *These* vampires were not monsters, and they didn't deserve to die here because of her.

She looked at the werewolf, Patrick. He was dangerous, but he needed her. Could she trust that need and hope to leverage it, at least for time? Would time be enough for the others to get out? She had to think it would. She had to trust that if a vampire wasn't automatically evil, neither was a werewolf.

She touched Ian's arm, gaining his attention. He glared at her and shook his head, but she knew she had no choice. She gave him a soft smile and squared her shoulders, stepping in front of him, closer to Patrick. Ian reached out and put a possessive hand on her waist, but he didn't try to pull her behind him and his soft touch gave her confidence. "I'll go with you, Patrick, but you aren't leaving any wolves behind here. They all leave this place."

Ian hissed, and his grip on her waist tightened.

Patrick laughed, "Sure, we don't give a shit about Julie and her little clan. Let's go." He held up a gun and pointed it at Ian. "No one is rushing this doorway and getting out alive, so don't even think about it. Back up to the wall," he commanded.

"You don't have to do this," Ian said, turning Katherine and meeting her gaze.

His eyes were intense. She felt a thrill go through her at his concern. He wasn't trying to force her to do what he wanted, and that made her heart flutter even more. He didn't look at her like prey and he didn't want to own or devour her, but he cared for her deeply, wanted to protect her. This was what sweeping someone off their feet felt like, and she smiled up at him.

She reached up on tiptoes and he bent his head to meet her. She pressed her lips to his quickly. "I have to. I know you'll come for me soon. I trust you, Ian."

She moved before he could respond and walked to the waiting wolf, who was grinning like he'd just won the lottery.

"Great choice. See you all in hell." He opened the cell door and Katherine walked through. No one attempted to escape with her. It wasn't worth risking one of their deaths, not at this point anyway and she was glad. She threw one last look over her shoulder and trembled at the sight of Ian's face twisted into rage. His fangs were bared, and his eyes were completely black. His hands were fisted at his sides and Beltar stood behind him, a hand on his shoulder offering support. She wondered if that connection was the only thing holding him back. Most surprising was the look of death on Prat and Trenton's faces. They didn't even know her, but they looked like they had been seconds from attacking Patrick if the fact that Laric had a hand over each one's throat was any indication. She turned away and hurried up the stairs before she broke down. The last thing she wanted was to show Patrick her tears.

"You're really making the only choice, dear. Don't feel bad. We'd have happily killed you if you hadn't agreed. Since it seems everyone already thinks you're dead, what would be the harm?"

He spoke casually of her death, and it sent a shot of fear through her. "How do you know that?" She asked between gritted teeth. As much as she'd like to yell at him or ignore him, she was sure that whatever information she could get from him would only benefit her situation.

"You weren't on our radar until the break in. We have a source in Miami that keeps an eye out for anything unusual because we don't venture down that way. It's far too close to the vamps' territory, but when we heard that Norgis had been released and stole something quite valuable, or so the Descendants think, we started thinking. Perhaps something valuable to us could have ended up in a museum somewhere."

"Like a bone to chew," she couldn't help scoffing.

His laugh surprised her.

They'd made it to Julie's office doorway and Chase stood there looking smug. "Have fun with the wolves," he sneered.

"Have fun getting your throat ripped out by a vampire," she hissed back. His eyes showed a second of fear before he covered it with bravado.

"As if," was his weak reply, and she smiled, knowing she'd hit him in his fear spot.

She turned to Patrick and noticed his gaze was devouring the wall of books in Julie's office.

"Chase! Get in here!" Julie snapped from behind her desk.

"Mother calls," Katherine sneered, and followed Patrick the rest of the way out of the house.

The entire pack was waiting for them, all in human form now, most only partially dressed. "You guys can't afford shirts?" she scoffed.

"What's the matter, too much male for you?" Patrick laughed and strode forward to the hoots and congratulations of the others. He was a victorious leader.

Then it hit her, they were *all* male. An uneasy feeling overtook her.

"Where are the female wolves? You don't trust them to attack vampires with wooden splinter bullets?"

A brief look of emotion flashed over Patrick's face before he caught it and replaced it with blankness. "Female wolves are extremely rare. The transition is a very violent and painful process. Only the strongest survive the attack and subsequent change." He opened the passenger door of a black sedan and motioned for her to get in.

Two wolves got in the back seat and Patrick took the driver's seat. The rest of the pack took off on foot, heading back home, she assumed. At least they were following that piece of negotiation. Although she had a feeling it had been their plan anyway, she was fooling herself if she thought she'd really told Patrick what to do. The mission that involved her from here must not warrant any extra muscle. That was probably a good sign for her ultimate survival. As if she had a chance against three werewolves, or one. She was no martial artist, and she didn't own a gun.

"So, what are you after at the museum?" she asked as the gates of the Descendants' compound disappeared behind them. She needed a distraction, needed to not think about the painful pull that was happening in her body as she got farther and farther from Ian. Was it the blood? Or was it something deeper?

"A Blood Moonstone," Patrick said with awe.

"Blood Moonstone?"

"When there's a full moon, we are forced to change," he explained. "Forced to lose ourselves to the animal almost completely. It's a fun time. We run, we hunt," he looked at her slyly. "When there were females, we would fuck."

She refused to show any reaction to his obvious bait. "But..." she prodded.

"But if we are caught at home, if we try, and stay close to our human loved ones because we think this time will be different, that we will have more control," his words were bitter, and his hands gripped the wheel tightly. "We risk hunting and killing the ones we love the most, the humans who have pledged their lives to us, the children they have borne for us." He gave a bitter laugh. "You'd think love would be enough, but the wolf doesn't recognize human emotions."

Patrick's voice was low and so full of emotion she nearly gasped. Tears stung her eyes as she realized what he was saying, the horror that must be their existence. No wonder they seemed a little more than half crazy. She looked out into the dark woods, unsure of what to think of them now. A movement in the trees caught her eye briefly, and she thought she caught a whiff of decay. *Norgis?* She wondered. Would Jovi do anything to save his brother? She dared to hope and feared the worst.

Fourteen

IAN WAS GOING TO EXPLODE. He was going to rip apart everyone in this cell and he was going to tear into whoever opened the door next. He didn't care about the consequences.

"Ian," Beltar said quietly. "You have to calm yourself. We will get out of here and we will get to her. She's safe for now. They need her."

Beltar's words did little to ease him. Many things could happen to her while they kept her alive enough to help; and when, when would they get out of here? It could so quickly become too late, and he wasn't sure he could keep going if he lost her before he even really had her.

The twins paced with irritation at the back of the cell as if they agreed with his assessment that this was all bullshit. He appreciated their support. Laric was glowering and Ian knew he was plotting, but he couldn't see any way to get out, not in time. Samson stared at Sorcha from across the cell and Sorcha pretended to ignore all of them as she stared out at the stairway.

"Julie better get her ass down here and let us go soon, or she's going to have a problem," Sorcha said. She walked to the door and gripped the bars, yelling up the stairs. She continued like that for an hour, to no avail.

The vampires brooded. None of them had their full strength back and they couldn't risk another serious injury so soon, making their options for escape limited. They needed blood. Trenton suggested they partake in whatever Sorcha might have in her body to speed the healing process, which was met by outrage from Samson, who nearly tore through Beltar and Ian in an effort to get to Trenton.

Sorcha just snapped at them all for being *animals*.

"Relax, we aren't taking Sorcha's blood," Beltar assured his friend. "Anyone else who comes down though..." Beltar added quietly as noise above them started to get louder.

Screams and shouts were followed by crashing and even a couple of gunshots. No one moved as they stared at the ceiling, trying to track the noise through the house above.

"What the fuck?" Sorcha said, stepping away from the bars.

Samson hurried to her side and the way she clung to his arm sent a flare of longing through Ian.

"Do you think the werewolves turned on the Descendants?" Prat asked.

"Could be, but I don't hear any growling or howling," Beltar said thoughtfully. "Maybe they really did leave the compound."

Things upstairs went quiet then, and moments later, the door at the top of the stairs opened. The smell of Norgis floated down, assaulting their nostrils and then Jovi's voice. "Hello prisoners," he greeted.

With a bright, smiling face, Julie sauntered down the stairs in front of Jovi. She looked like she'd been dragged across the yard. There were leaves in her hair, grass stains on her jeans, and dirty scratches along one cheek. But she seemed to not care one bit as she reached the door and put the key in the lock, but not turning it. "Hey guys," she said brightly.

"What the fuck," Sorcha whispered.

"You know, it's a funny thing about Norgis," Jovi said with a grin from behind Julie. "He's dumb."

The beast made a growl sort of noise beside Jovi.

"Which is quite useful for following orders, but also for walking through spells meant to target a part of the mind. He could see right through the spell covering this place and once in, he was able to quickly dismantle the spell and expose this place to the world," Jovi said triumphantly.

It finally made sense; this was why Jovi had chosen Norgis. His simple mind could see through the complex spell hiding the Descendants.

Ian eyed the key stuck in the lock eagerly. There was no way Jovi was going to be able to kill them all if that's what he planned, and as soon as the door opened, Ian was on his way to Katherine. The wolves would suffer for harming her. Even now he could feel their connection, so much stronger since she'd taken more of his blood to save his life. She seemed to be asleep and unharmed as far as he could tell, but getting father away by the second.

"Open the door, *brother*," Ian growled.

"You'll leave, go get your little girlfriend, and leave the rest of the Descendants to me," Jovi commanded.

"Yes," Ian agreed quickly. He cared only about one Descendant, the others he'd worry about later.

"You won't touch Sorcha," Samson growled at Jovi.

Jovi smiled. "Of course not! Don't you see? Don't you all understand? I want what we have so long been denied. These people were meant to be our everything and we deserve to find them and take them, to have them care for us and feed us. I don't want to deny you the pleasure of their company. I want to gift you the pleasure of their servitude."

His words were so confident it made Ian sick; this was what his father had been trying to prevent by putting him in charge instead of Jovi. He suddenly felt like a failure. He should have gone after Jovi years ago to prevent this. He'd known what Jovi was after when he left, he just never believed he'd find it. Had believed the Descendants had destroyed it, not hidden it.

"Father would be ashamed," Ian whispered.

"Father was a fool! He lost all sense for what the world could be, didn't even fight back when the Descendants betrayed us." Jovi stepped forward and narrowed his eyes at Ian. "He let his heart believe they were worthy of their own minds, don't make the same mistake, Ian. Let your blood drain from her system and bring her under the control of the Stone before she leaves you."

Ian didn't react. He knew he had to hold himself in check or Jovi wasn't going to open that door and Ian could do nothing behind those bars, spelled against escape. "I don't want to control her and take away what she is, who she is," Ian said firmly.

Jovi laughed. "Just like Father, such a fool. He appointed *you* successor because he saw his own weakness mirrored in you. You didn't even take it on fully, you spit on the honor he gave you. You still call yourself prince and you treat the others as equals, call them friends and brothers." Jovi's voice had risen, and spit flew from his mouth as his anger rose with it. "You could have changed everything, you could have made it right, but you were weak, you *are* weak, and that is why I'll let you out. Go get her and take her to Atlantis. That's the only way you'll ever be able to keep her. She is a Descendant, and she was bred to serve you. But listen carefully, *brother*. If you don't leave the land with her, I will find her and I will command her to be mine. You'll have to watch her serve me, or you will have to kill her yourself." Jovi's threats were laced with a truth that clenched at Ian's heart.

As long as Jovi held that Stone, he could make Katherine his as soon as the vampire blood in her system worked its way out. The torture of that would be worse than anything. It was this fear, this truth, which held him back as the door opened and Jovi's sly smile challenged him. If Jovi somehow managed to kill him, Katherine would be in the worst kind of danger.

Ian raced out and up the stairs without another word or look for his brother. He didn't stop. He ran as fast as he could out of the house, across the yard, and through the gate. He would find her, and he would do whatever he had to do to make sure she was safe from the wolves, and Jovi, forever.

It had been a few days and Brandon hadn't been back down into the basement. He'd sent Glen down to feed her, but he couldn't shake the feeling of unease every time he passed the door that led down to her. Something had shifted.

But after a few days, his confidence had returned, and he was ready to prove himself.

"We're going hunting tonight," he declared as Glen walked into the shop at sunset.

"Gators?" Glen asked dumbly, and Brandon almost threw something at his idiot cousin.

"Not fucking gators, you dumbass. Vamps, we're hunting vamps tonight, so strap on some gear. I'll get the bitch ready."

"Fuck yeah!" Glen said with wild eyes.

When Brandon walked down the stairs, she was sitting up, looking at him as if she knew exactly what was about to happen. He had a sudden fearful thought. Could she hear what was said upstairs? Did she listen to everything that went on and was she conscious enough to process it? No, that was ridiculous. "Dumb bitch animal," he sneered as he grabbed the silver leash. "Time to do your job and hunt down some bloodsuckers."

She lifted her lips to flash her sharp teeth.

Brandon took that as agreement. She didn't move as he clicked the leash to her collar.

"Good bitch," he said with satisfaction, letting go of the worry of the last few days. He was in control, he was the human, the last of the Aristotle Society. She was nothing, just a dumb animal.

As soon as they were outside, she started to pull, not like she was trying to get away, but as if she had urgent business in a certain direction. He smiled at Glen and they were off, no doubt hot on the trail of a bloodsucker.

Fifteen

KATHERINE WOKE up as they entered the city. They hadn't stopped except for gas, snacks—werewolves eat a lot—and bathroom breaks. The sun was setting again, and they'd finally hit the city limits. Ian would be just getting up and she had a feeling he'd escaped the compound. The blood that rushed through her system kept them connected and she felt he was coming for her; she just wasn't sure he'd be in time. She'd barely felt him during the day. Had he bunkered in a basement? Slept through the sunlit hours? It would mean he was far behind and that scared her. She had to delay them as long as possible because once they didn't need her, she wouldn't count on them keeping her alive.

She'd gotten a little more explanation out of them on the ride. They wanted the Blood Moonstone. It had been lost or stolen, depending on who you asked, many years ago. Some say it was stolen by a secret society that used werewolves as weapons against vampires. The Aristotle Society they called themselves. The group was no longer active according to Patrick, but the Stone had never surfaced. They wanted her to not only search through the museum itself, but in the databases she had access to of other museum's collections. It felt like a long shot, but she was willing to do anything to get these guys to not kill her.

"You know, if I can't find anything right away, I might be able to contact some people I know, dig deeper. It could take time," she pointed out as the city loomed before them.

"Time I can give you," Patrick said quietly, and the other two grunted agreement.

She hoped he could give her a lot. It wouldn't be easy to make contact as a supposedly dead woman. "We can't go in the museum until everyone leaves for the night. They think I'm dead. If I show up, it won't be a small ordeal," she said as if she wanted nothing more than to be helpful.

Patrick frowned, but nodded. "You're probably right. We can kill a few hours, eat, and then go in when it's empty." He pulled over and one of the other wolves jumped out of the car. Tray was his name, she'd learned, and the other was Dallas. Tray was quiet and thoughtful, brooding and Dallas was a loud mouth, always with something to say and thought himself to be very funny.

"Tray, you let us know as soon as it's empty or nearly so, we can handle a few humans if we have to, no problem," Patrick instructed.

That didn't settle with Katherine very well, but she had little choice, so she kept her mouth shut. They continued on as Tray disappeared, loping down a side street too fast and smooth to be human. When they stopped at a burger place, Katherine had thoughts of trying to escape but quickly dismissed them. She could run to the police and tell them what? She'd been attacked by a monster that had escaped from Atlantis, was saved by a vampire, held captive by the Descendants of Atlantis, then kidnapped by a bunch of werewolves! Yeah, she'd find help; straight into a hospital and handcuffed to a bed for her own safety.

So she sat at a table and nibbled a chicken sandwich while Patrick and Dallas scarfed down three burgers each, plus fries, onion rings and milkshakes. It was a disgusting amount of food and gained them a few looks from the waitresses, but no one commented.

By the time they were leaving the restaurant, it was full dark and the pull of Ian was strong. It was like a warm knowing; he was getting closer and fast. She had to try and delay the trip to the museum as long as possible. When they got to the car, she paused and gave Patrick a grimace. "Oh, I need to hit the ladies." He looked doubtful, so she crossed her knees and whined a little. "I think the mayo was bad on my sandwich."

He growled a little, but nodded. "Follow her," he ordered Dallas. As if she could possibly run from a couple of werewolves.

Katherine smiled thankfully and waddle-ran to the bathroom as if she was worried she wouldn't make it. When the door closed behind her, she relaxed. This wasn't going to buy a lot of time, but it was a start. She glanced around, frantic for an idea. She thought about dousing her clothing with water and begging to go to her apartment and change, but he would likely just say no. She could try to escape knowing she wouldn't get far and hope they didn't kill her for the trouble, but she wasn't sure she was willing to risk that they needed her that badly and there was a lot of hurt they could dish out without actually killing her. So she sat and waited until Dallas started banging on the door and threatening to come in and get her if she didn't hurry up.

She flushed and washed her hands and walked out with what she hoped was an embarrassed look on her face. "Jeez, can't a girl use the bathroom in your world?"

"Not when she's trying to buy time in the hopes that her vampire boyfriend will show up and save the day," he growled.

"He's not my boyfriend," she said, her cheeks reddening and ignoring the accusation of trying to delay.

Dallas just grunted and pushed her forward. When they met Patrick at the car, he was smiling.

"Tray says the place cleared out!"

"Oh good, no time to waste now," Dallas said, looking at

Katherine meaningfully. She just rolled her eyes and got in the car, as if she had a choice.

"You know I have no problem giving you guys the Stone, so you don't kill your loved ones," she said with a huff. "I am not pro-killing anyone."

"But..." Patrick prodded with a half grin.

"But if you think you can kill me after, we have a problem, *you* have a problem because Ian won't stand for that shit."

"I thought he wasn't your boyfriend," Dallas teased from the backseat.

"He's not, but he *is* inexplicably protective of me, and he'll be really mad if I die."

"Vampires get that way about their pets," Dallas said with a laugh.

Katherine clenched her jaw and refused to respond. A few minutes later, they were parked behind the museum. The police tape was gone, and it looked eerily normal, as if she hadn't been murdered in there, as if her life hadn't been altered to such an extreme in there. It looked as if they'd all just moved on. They accepted that they were never going to know what happened to her, never going to be able to explain the blood and damage with no body or evidence of another human involved.

Was she so unimportant? The thought made her gut clench and tears burn her eyes; how can someone disappear with so little ripple in the real world?

"You okay?" Patrick asked with surprising gentleness, bringing her out of her depressing thoughts.

"Fine," she hissed and jumped out of the car. She'd made no mark with her life so far and that knowledge made her even more determined to survive this night and do something, anything, that had meaning with her life. She was done feeling sorry for herself for being adopted, for being an average student, average employee, average fiancée that had ended up with a predictable breakup and since then, a less than average person.

She'd had plans. Growing up, she'd been determined to make discoveries, to be the female Indiana Jones! She was going to go to exotic places and unearth artifacts. She was going to change the ideas of history because of what she found. She was going to make a name for herself in academic circles. Classes would study her as an example to follow.

She wasn't going to sit in a museum going through other people's discoveries. That hadn't been the plan when she started out. She'd taken the job, loved the job and immersed herself in it so she wouldn't realize that it wasn't her goal, it wasn't what she'd wanted her life to be.

As she strode toward the familiar building and the blood of a vampire coursed through her body, telling her Ian was getting closer, she knew she had the potential to be more than average and that knowledge gave her enough confidence to know that no matter what, she would survive this night. Norgis hadn't killed her, werewolves wouldn't either, and she really, *really* wanted to see what would happen if she let these feelings of desire she had for Ian loose.

Tray ran across the lot and met them with a grin. "All clear, let's do this!"

"The door will be locked. I have a key in my apartment, it isn't far," Katherine said, hoping to delay again.

"We don't need a key," Patrick said and grabbed the door handle, ripping it half off its hinges with little visible effort.

"So I guess you guys aren't into stealth," she mumbled.

She was shocked to find the warehouse was cleaned up. The floor that had been covered in pieces of artifacts was swept clear, washed of her blood too, and all the bits and pieces of her work were laid out on tables ready for labeling and storage. That would have been her job, and she would have loved every second of it. Now she shuddered at the memories of this place and felt thankful that she wasn't going to spend the next six months of her life in this lightless room hunched over tables of artifacts. Working alone, touching the past that other people discovered instead of living in the present and making her own discoveries.

She wasn't sure she wanted to come back from the dead and reclaim her former life. Would Ian offer her a part of his? Did she want that? She bit her lip as desire and nerves wrapped around her stomach. What would that be like, and could she survive it?

"Where do we start?" Patrick snapped when she just stood there, gathering her thoughts.

"Does it look like I know?" she snapped back, annoyed that while she was trying to figure out if she might want a future with a vampire that was sweeping her off her feet, she was being pushed around by werewolves threatening her life. "Norgis and Jovi did a number on this place." She walked over to the tables and started searching for anything that looked like it might be or hold a stone. "And I wasn't here to clean up and organize," she grumbled, already noticing that whoever had done this hadn't done it the way she would have. She knew it wouldn't be with this stuff. It was all much older than what Patrick had described, but it would delay and she was sure that was what she needed to do.

A growl at the door had them all turning with surprise. An emaciated wolf was there, leashed and held back by a man who looked like he belonged behind a display full of comic books and card games. Tall and skinny, greasy hair and an old leather jacket. His shorts had little Spiderman emblems all over them and his boots looked like they'd seen better days. This guy looked out of his league, and she didn't think he was more than he appeared. Right behind him stood a man that matched him for idiot of the year. Shaved blond hair and a gaping mouth showing at least one missing tooth. He wore a dirty tank top and cutoff shorts. His boots were untied, but he had weapons strapped to his body and Katherine was not going to underestimate them.

She heard the others gasp around her. "What the fuck is that?" Dallas said with awe clear in his voice, surprising her.

"A female, how the fuck do you have a female?" Patrick

growled at the human. The words sounding more animal than human, and Katherine stepped back.

"She's tracking a vamp. Where is the bloodsucker?" the man demanded, holding up a handgun. His partner pulled up a gun too, following the leader, apparently.

"No, she's tracking an alpha," Patrick said, his eyes locked onto her, and she was looking back at him, teeth bared. "She looks half dead!" Patrick snarled.

Katherine noticed Patrick's body start to ripple. His hands were clenched, and she took another step back. If he was about to wolf out, she didn't want to be anywhere near him.

The three werewolf men stepped forward, and the man pulled back on the chain he held, making the wolf yip. The werewolves froze immediately at the sound of pain from the female, all three of them gasping in anger.

"Take another step and I'll shoot," the man threatened. "Where's the vamp?"

"No vamps here, boy. Who the hell are you?" Patrick demanded.

"Brandon, leader of the Aristotle Society and handler of this weapon," he yanked the chain again. "This is my cousin, Glen." He motioned with his head to the man standing slightly behind him.

"Aristotle Society!" Dallas gasped. "I thought you were gone."

"Not gone and not interested in lies. I don't give a shit about you wolves; we hunt vamps, and she led me here, so what the hell is *she*?" He pointed his gun at Katherine and she took a step back.

"Human!" Katherine said quickly, holding up her hands.

"I want one," Glen said, his eyes wide as he looked at the three men.

"Idiot," Katherine hissed. Did this man actually think he was going to be able to capture and keep one of these werewolves? It was stupidity beyond even what his number of teeth indicated.

"Where's the vamp then?" Brandon demanded.

"She might just smell the vampire scent on me," Katherine explained quickly, hoping to defuse the situation.

"A vampire whore?" Brandon sneered and raised his gun. "A good enough reason for me."

The next things happened fast. The gun shot, Dallas jumped to push her out of the way and Tray lunged for the men. A second later, Katherine was struggling for breath on the hard ground, not sure she hadn't been shot and the sound of snarling and fighting reverberated around the warehouse.

Beside her, Dallas lay unconscious, and she quickly realized he'd taken a shot in the back. Katherine jumped to him. These werewolves might be assholes, but they were just after something to keep their families safe, she couldn't really hold that against them. They could have been nicer about it, but she knew she couldn't just let him die; he'd just saved her life.

"Is he dead?" Patrick asked, rushing over.

Katherine felt Dallas' neck. There was a pulse. "No, but he got hit, and he's definitely bleeding. He needs a hospital."

"Werewolves don't survive hospitals," Patrick said with a frown, then turned to the doorway where things had suddenly gone quiet.

The female werewolf was staring down at Tray. He'd shifted into a large red wolf and lay in front of her, not fighting, just watching her as she snarled at him. Brandon was holding his arm that had held the gun, his hand mangled and she was pretty sure he was missing a finger or two. She couldn't help being glad about that. Glen was gone, must have taken off when things got difficult. She wasn't surprised.

"She'll tear his throat out if you so much as move," Brandon said with a shaky voice that lacked all confidence. Then Glen returned and stood behind Brandon, holding up a gun. Katherine didn't move.

"What do you want?" Patrick growled.

"We won't kill that bitch, for now. But we're keeping this

wolf." He motioned to Tray. "These two can breed us some nice pups, can't they, Glen?"

"Sure as shit!" Glen said with an accent that made Katherine think of a gator farm on the bayou. He turned and spat out a black mass that made her gag.

"I suggest you start making new friends if you want to keep breathing. I won't hesitate to kill you next time I come around and you're smelling like you've been with a bloodsucker," Brandon threatened.

Patrick shifted into a large black wolf and stood before her with bared fangs.

"Shit, he's huge!" Glen said, taking a step back, his gun trembling.

Coward, Katherine thought.

"Just get a collar on this male," Brandon ordered. "I need to get stitched." Obviously, Brandon could see the dangerous situation they were in. Dallas was starting to wake up and two pissed wolves against them probably wasn't a fair match even if they did still have one gun.

Glen hurried to comply, collaring Tray with ease. Katherine wasn't sure why the wolf wasn't fighting back, but it wasn't her concern. She was having a hard enough time keeping herself alive through all of this. Soon Brandon and Glen were backing out with Tray on a leash, his eyes watching the female intensely, and it made Katherine think of the way she'd seen Samson watch Sorcha.

"Be safe brother," Patrick whispered after shifting back to human.

Katherine tried to keep her eyes off Patrick's now naked body and turned back to Dallas, who was still bleeding. "What do we do?"

"Find the fucking Stone so we can get out of here. All that noise is bound to call attention to us, and I don't need a run in with the police. Dallas will be fine soon enough. The bullet wouldn't have done a thing if he'd thought to shift before blocking it. Our skin is much less penetrable when we're in wolf form."

She wasn't sure how to respond. She wanted to ask about Tray but apparently Patrick wasn't worried about his friend's capture, so she just went back to searching while Patrick inspected Dallas' wound. As Patrick had predicted, he woke up grunting and groaning after a couple minutes.

"I need to do a search of the computer database. I need to go through the museum itself, but it will take time. I can do it, but your friend looks like he needs attention now," Katherine pointed out.

"He'll be fine, search," Patrick demanded.

Katherine wanted to argue, but she didn't, just hurried to the sections of the museum she thought might be the right time period and brought a few things to Patrick, who said no quickly with a deep disappointment.

"I really think I might be able to email a few people with a description, but it's not going to be answered tonight," she explained. "I swear I will, I want to help," she said with a shrug. She really did despite them kidnapping her. "I owe Dallas my life," she added.

Patrick nodded, "Maybe we won't have to eat you after all," he said with a wink.

"Gee thanks, can I go now? I'll call you when I hear something," she snarked, no longer afraid of these werewolves.

"Just one more thing. You said your apartment is near?"

"Yeah," she said cautiously.

"Do you have a sewing kit?"

She sighed dramatically. "Yeah, unless someone's packed up the dead girl's apartment already," she grumbled.

Sixteen

BRANDON COULDN'T BELIEVE his luck! He may not have popped his vampire cherry, but he'd secured a male werewolf. He was going to do what his father and grandfather had always dreamed of. He was going to breed himself an army of vampire slayers. He rode a high unlike anything he'd ever shot up, snorted, or smoked, and it was enough to dull the pain of his missing digits for a time.

"Do you really think they'll do it?" Glen asked as he shut the van door and hopped into the driver's seat.

"If they don't want to, we make them," Brandon said with a laugh. The female whined in the back and the male growled. Brandon hit the bars that separated the men from the beasts with his good hand and laughed again. "Don't act like you won't enjoy it, you little bitch."

Glen laughed as he pulled out of the parking lot. "Why didn't they come after their friend?" he wondered out loud as they pulled away from the pawn shop.

Brandon guffawed, "Dumb dogs probably don't have any loyalty to each other, and besides, they could tell who was in control!" Brandon puffed out his chest. "No one messes with the men of the Aristotle Society." Brandon frowned at his bloody hand. "I hope your sister is home and can take care of this hand."

"Yeah, she doesn't strip on Wednesdays, so she should be."

There was silence in the back and Brandon looked back at their prize. The bitch was licking the male's face. "Oh good, she likes him," he said with a laugh.

The male's eyes lifted and met his. A spike of fear laced through Brandon and he shuddered, quickly looking away. There was something raw in those eyes and the way the female was cuddled up to the male as if he would protect her, it made Brandon break out in a sweat.

"I think I've lost too much blood," he said, wiping his forehead. He was imagining things again. They were just dumb animals.

Glen stepped on the gas, and they sped down the highway.

Ian arrived in Miami an hour before sunrise. He followed the pull of Katherine to her apartment; she was alive, but was she safe? The smell of wolf was strong here, and blood, wolf blood. He didn't know what to expect, so he listened outside the door, but he heard nothing. Then there was the quiet pad of feet on carpet, and the door flung open.

Katherine stood there, eyes wide and hair a mess. She was wearing an oversized t-shirt and shorts. She looked amazing. He wanted to wrap her in his arms and never let go, but he was afraid to touch her, afraid she was harmed, afraid danger lurked behind her in the dark somewhere.

"Are you safe?"

She nodded with a small smile, blinking against the light from the hallway.

"Did I wake you?" he asked with a laugh when he realized there was no one else moving or breathing in the apartment.

She flung herself into his arms and he forgot all of his fear as she pressed her lips to his. "I knew you'd come," she said against his mouth.

He walked into the apartment and shut the door behind him with a foot. "Katherine," he whispered as she continued to kiss his mouth, his chin, his neck. Leaving a little path of fire that was more delightful than anything he'd ever experienced. "Where are the wolves? I smell them, and their blood."

"They left," she said, laying a kiss to his lips again.

"Left?" He couldn't hide his astonishment.

"Yeah, I didn't find the Stone, but I'm going to do a little research, see if I can. I stitched up a gunshot wound, and they left."

"Wait," he said firmly, putting her down on the ground and holding her away from him. "What happened?" he demanded quietly.

She gave a frustrated sound that almost made him melt ,then started talking. "We went to the museum, and we were searching for this Stone, a Blood Moonstone. Well, these guys came in with a wolf on a leash!"

"Aristotle Society," Ian said darkly.

"Yeah! What the hell is that?"

"They are vampire hunters, at least they were. I believed they'd died out a long time ago, but apparently there's one left behind."

"Two," she corrected.

"Okay, two. The one I met doesn't seem to really know what he's doing, but he has a werewolf to track vampires and a gun that shoots wooden bullets."

"Thank God they don't splinter like the other ones did! Dallas took one to the back saving me, and we had to pry that sucker out and stitch up the hole."

"He saved you," Ian said with a raised eyebrow, jealousy welling up hot and fierce. No one should protect her but him.

"Yeah, I guess they really were just after using me for the Stone.

I'm no threat to them and I'm useful. I'll find it if I can." She shrugged as if it were nothing unusual.

"No, you are no threat," he said with a grin. She was small and weak and beautiful, and she was all his to protect. He reached out and touched her chin. "Katherine, the sun will be up any moment. Is there a light tight space here I can bunk for the day?"

"Oh," she said, surprise lighting up her features, quickly followed by a little disappointment. "You should be safe in the bathroom; it doesn't have any windows and you can shove a towel at the bottom of the door just to be sure."

He leaned forward and kissed her gently. "Please don't leave before I come back out."

"Where would I go?" she said with a laugh. "I'm dead, remember."

"I'm serious this time. Don't leave." He hated to order her around, but he couldn't take any chances with her, not while Jovi and Norgis were still out there.

Katherine nodded without argument, and it filled him with relief. He hurried into the bathroom, hating that he couldn't be with her right now, hating that she was out there and possibly vulnerable. And he plotted ways to convince her to go with him to Atlantis and live under the ocean away from the sun for an eternity.

He listened to her move about all morning and was comforted by the knowledge that she was safe within this apartment. She wasn't quiet, and he wondered what she was doing. When she knocked quietly on the door, he was a bit surprised.

"Yes?"

"Um, this is sort of embarrassing," she said quietly.

"What is?" he asked, confused.

"Well, you're in my bathroom."

"I am," he said with realization.

"Well," she paused, and he could hear her taking a breath. "I need to use it."

"Oh, that's nothing to be embarrassed about. That is life. I had one once," he added as an afterthought.

"I think I made the bedroom light tight. I taped up plastic garbage bags and blankets."

"How thoughtful," he said with a sly grin. The fact that she'd chosen the bedroom and not the living room made his thighs twitch. He opened the door and squinted. The light filtering down the hall from the living room was enough to disturb his sensitive eyes and feel hot on his skin.

"That way," she said quickly, pushing him down the hall and into the bedroom. She shut the door when he was inside and moments later, he heard the bathroom door shut as well.

When she knocked on the bedroom door a while later, he was lounging on her bed, enjoying the scent of her surrounding him. It held a hint of himself now since she'd taken more of his blood so recently. He could admit to himself how much he loved that; it filled in a deep need of possession he never thought he'd have.

"It's your house, Katherine. You don't need permission to enter the bedroom."

"I wasn't sure if you would be awake," she admitted shyly.

"If I had been asleep, your knock would have woken me," he said with a laugh.

She looked embarrassed, and he sat up. "You may interrupt my sleep any time. What do you need?"

"Need? Oh, well..." she looked nervous, and it made him smile.

Whatever her mind was trying to grapple with had her twisted up and he wondered which side of her was going to win. "Yes?" he asked, his voice gone gruff as his mind wandered to the things he wanted her to ask him.

"Can I sleep with you?"

He grinned and laid back down, patting the bed.

"It's just been a really long couple of days and I'm exhausted," she said as she laid down with her back to him. "Maybe I'm turning into a night owl," she said with a laugh.

"I would never deny you sleep," he said, pulling her close and kissing the top of her head.

They did sleep then. Ian dreamed of walking the streets of Atlantis with her by his side, introducing her as his wife, his mate, his everything. Everyone would be jealous, and it filled him with pride.

Seventeen

KATHERINE WOKE to Ian kissing her neck. At first she stiffened, thinking he was about to bite her, but he just left gentle kisses on her skin. A sigh escaped her lips, and he lifted his head to grin down at her. His teeth flashed white in the dark, and she wasn't even afraid to see his fangs. She trusted him completely.

"Good evening, Katherine."

"Is the sun down?"

"Just about."

"We need to go back and help the others. How did you get out, what—oh!" Her words were cut off by his hand moving between her thighs.

"Katherine, my love. I desire you beyond measure. Will you allow me to claim you as my own?"

His words took her breath away and she could only nod agreement as her heart fluttered. His grin was lascivious and everything he did from there was designed to wring pleasure from every part of her body.

He touched her as if he was afraid she would break, and his gaze was intense, investigating every inch of her. She'd never felt so seen before and instead of making her self-conscious, she gloried in his appraisal. He kissed her skin softly and made sounds of pleasure as he found a mole here and there.

"You are exquisite," he mumbled as he pressed his lips to her neck once again.

She lay before him, naked and frustrated. He still had his clothes on, and she wanted to see him, wanted to touch him like he was touching her. She reached up to pull his shirt from his pants and he grinned as she wrestled it off of him. "Take these off," she demanded, tugging on the waistband of his jeans.

"Yes, ma'am," he said with a wink. He hopped off the bed and was back in a flash, fully nude and very erect.

"Everything works the same?" she asked, a little breathless.

"Yes," he assured her as she let her hands follow her eyes over his muscles.

"You're exquisite," she said with a grin.

"We make a perfect pair then, don't we?"

"Absolutely," she agreed and pulled him down for another kiss.

He moved between her thighs and pressed against her.

She moaned and lifted her hips in invitation. He took it, diving in with one swift, smooth stroke.

She gasped and broke the kiss. Her hands gripped his shoulders, and he didn't move a muscle as her body adjusted to the size of him. After a moment, she started to move beneath him, and he captured her lips again as his body began a slow methodical assault on her, inside and out.

It wasn't long before she was screaming his name and he flipped them as she settled, bringing her on top while she was still shuddering. "Take what you want," he demanded, as she gave him a hesitant look.

She gathered confidence from the look of desire in his eyes and began to move on him. Her hands gripping his chest, the bed, and his thighs at different times. She felt reckless and wanton, everything the women in her romance novels seemed to be, and she loved every second of it. When the second orgasm hit, she was loud and unashamed. He pulled her to him and flipped them again, holding her to his body as he slammed into her hard and fast, grunting out his own release and just as she thought it was over, his fangs slipped into her neck, a quick nip, no real pain and he tugged at her vein, sending a thrill through her body and a third orgasm so intense she thought she might have blacked out at the end.

When she could see straight again, she was cuddled up against Ian's hard body. Ian was breathing slowly; his fingers running up and down her arm gently and he was staring up at the ceiling with an indecipherable look on his face.

Fear coursed through her suddenly. Did he regret what they'd done? She turned from him and tried to slide away before she did something really stupid like cry.

"Where do you think you're going, woman?" he said with a voice so low and deep she shivered. He pulled her against him and kissed her neck where he had bitten her. "I'm sorry," he said quietly.

"Oh, well, don't worry, it was my fault. I threw myself at you. I should have just slept on the couch out there and left you alone." He did regret it. She wanted to die, wanted the bed to swallow her, she wanted to disappear.

He laughed then, a low rumble.

He fucking laughed at her shame! She reared up and slapped him. How dare he laugh at her. He grabbed her and twisted. She was on her back and he was looming above her with mirth all over his face.

"You're an asshole," she snapped. If she stayed angry, she wouldn't cry.

"You think I am apologizing for fucking you?"

She didn't answer, just bit her lip.

"I am apologizing for the love bite. I should have asked before I took from you. I'm sorry."

His face showed true regret, and it softened her to him even more. "Oh, no apologies necessary I... well, I liked it," she said with face flaming.

"I know," he said with a sly grin. "But I want you to know that it's not something I take lightly. It is a gift from you that I cherish, and I would never want to take from you something you were not happy to give."

His words were full of emotion and truth, and it filled her with something damn close to love, and it scared her a little. "Thank you," she said, not sure there was anything else to say. He was the farthest thing from a monster, vampire or not.

"Will you come to Atlantis with me?"

She bit her lip and thought. She had no job, no life really, everyone assumed she was dead. "Sure, why not," she said with only a hint of hysteria in her voice. It was what she'd hoped he would ask her and feared he would at the same time. "Who wouldn't want a vacation in Atlantis," she added with a laugh.

His genuine smile smoothed out her worries, and she was suddenly excited. She was going to see the lost city of Atlantis!

"What about your men, and your brother? Oh god what happened after I left? How did you get out?"

"Norgis," Ian said with a heavy sigh. "Jovi picked him because he's so simple minded the spell that keeps the Descendants' compound hidden doesn't work on him. He was able to get in and break the spell, then Jovi was able to get in and with the Stone he was able to take control rather quickly, of course." Ian's words were bitter, and she reached out to put a comforting hand on his arm.

Katherine wasn't sure how she felt about those people being enslaved. They were insane, and hadn't been kind to her, but they didn't deserve to be anyone's blood slaves. "And just let you go?" she said doubtfully.

"He did."

"Why?"

Ian looked thoughtful for a moment. "I think because he

doesn't believe I've got what it takes. He does truly believe he's stronger than me and that is going to be his biggest mistake. That's why I need to get back to Atlantis. I need to get some help to go up against Jovi. I'm strong enough to admit when I need help."

"Oh, will it be dangerous? Going up against Jovi?" Katherine couldn't help the spike of fear in her voice. She didn't want to lose him now that she had him, it was too soon.

"I will keep you safe," he promised her, and kissed her to seal it.

"I'm not worried about me," she said with a laugh when he pulled back and she felt like squirming with the desire he so easily flicked to life inside of her. She wondered briefly if it would always be like this, or if it was only due to the recent blood she'd taken from him.

"I'm a warrior, Katherine. You don't have to worry about me."

She giggled as he stood up and flexed for her.

"Now come, my woman, I wish to take you to Atlantis." He proclaimed, hands on hips and chin high.

"Okay, warrior man, I want a shower first. What does one wear to Atlantis? How do we get there? Is it far?" She had so many questions!

He laughed and grabbed her hand, pulling her up off the bed. "All will be answered. Go shower and dress to get wet."

"Is there wifi?" she asked with a frown. That last statement sounded ominous.

They made it to the edge of the water around midnight. Katherine had put on a sleek black one-piece swimsuit under a long sundress. She wasn't sure she'd have anything more to wear in Atlantis and didn't want to risk wearing one of her sexier two pieces for however long they might be down there. She knew Ian preferred a kilt and no shirt, but that didn't really tell her what women wore down there. She couldn't bring a computer, no wifi, he said. So her research would have to wait and she hoped the werewolves would be patient.

"I'm not a strong swimmer," she said carefully. She was confident in a normal scenario, but what she imagined this was going to be felt overwhelming.

"Don't worry, you won't have to swim the whole way," he said with a laugh and pointed.

She looked and saw a small fishing boat tied to a dock. "You want to steal a boat?"

He shrugged. "Unless you're a great swimmer, I think it's the best option. Besides, we are only borrowing it, really. It'll drift back to shore somewhere and be returned."

She couldn't argue with the necessity, so she went with it, feeling a bit like a criminal. It was a small boat, and he had no idea what to do to get it going, thankfully, she did. He started to look for oars and she just rolled her eyes and started the engine. Luckily, it was a pull start, and she had some experience with them. Her adopted dad had liked to fish, and they'd taken a similar boat out on the water nearly every weekend. Ian gave her a stunned look as she putted them out to sea, then settled in and directed her. He referenced the stars as he told her where to go, and every once in a while, he stuck his hand in the water as if he were testing it for something.

After only about twenty minutes, he apparently felt something he liked and told her to stop the boat.

"Here?" she asked, looking around at the empty water all around them. Zero indication of anything special here.

"Yes, this is the entrance. I can feel it in the water, and I can see it in the stars. This is where we start to swim."

"Down," she said carefully, peering over the edge of the boat into nothing but black water reflecting the stars above.

"Down," he confirmed, then stood and hopped over the side of the boat. He went under briefly and popped his head out with a smile, pushing his wet hair out of his face. "This is definitely the spot. I can feel the pull of the vortex."

"Vortex!" she said with alarm.

He laughed. "Come on, love. Don't be afraid. I promise you will be fine."

"Says the vampire," she grumbled, but she slid in as gently as she could.

"See, not so bad."

"For a night swim in the middle of the ocean, I suppose it's not so bad," she admitted. "But what's the word for the fear of swimming in water where you can't see the bottom? Because I definitely have that."

"Don't worry, I'm the biggest predator in this ocean," he grinned and flashed his fangs.

It should have scared her, she supposed, but all it did was make her tingle with anticipation. What was wrong with her?

He pushed the boat back toward land, then pulled her in for a kiss, seeming to have no trouble staying afloat. She felt a rise of panic as the boat drifted away.

"Katherine, I will always keep you safe," he promised and took her hand. "Now, follow me. We will swim fast and hard, straight down. The vortex will start to pull and when it does, things will go fast."

"You won't let go of me?"

"Of course not," he promised. "Now, take a deep breath."

She did, and then they were underwater and against every instinct, she was letting him drag her down toward the bottom. Soon her lungs began to burn, and panic swelled and just when she thought the panic might be too much, she felt a pull all over her body, a push behind her and a sucking in front. She was thrown through the water so fast she couldn't have stopped it if she'd wanted to. She stopped swimming and clung to Ian's arm with both hands. Her mind started to fuzz. She was desperate for air, and she was sure he was wrong. She couldn't do this, no human could. This was how she'd die. And with that thought came another, would she wake up like him? A vampire because of the blood of his she'd taken? The bite he'd given her in the heat of passion? What were the vampire making rules, she wondered dumbly as everything in her body sort of stopped feeling. Was that his plan? Drown her so she'd be like him? No, she knew that couldn't be it. He'd never do anything to her that she wasn't okay with.

Then a loud rushing sound hit her ears. Her skin tingled with an assault of bubbles and then Ian was dragging her out onto a sandy beach.

"Katherine! Katherine! Are you alright?" He asked in panic, shaking her shoulders.

Katherine opened her eyes and looked into his concerned gaze. "I died. Am I a vampire now?"

He chuckled and sat back. "It doesn't quite work that way. You survived; I didn't think it would be that hard on a human. I'll have to remember to take the shortcut next time."

"Shortcut!" she snapped and sat up, ready to pound him. But then she got a look at her surroundings, and she was speechless.

They were on a beach with white sand, warm underneath her. It was night and they were under the ocean, but somehow the sky above her was filled with bright stars. She looked back to where they'd come ashore, and it was an expanse of water seeming to go out forever. Farther up the beach was a line of palm trees and grass, bright flowers blooming even though it was night. But what really caught her attention was the enormous pyramid structure popping up beyond that. It looked straight out of Egypt and something resembling the Parthenon showed next to it too. It all looked perfectly preserved, no sign of decay or aging at all. It was an archeologist's dream. Her heart beat wildly.

"How—" was all she could manage.

"A few good spells," he said with a smile. "Come, I'll show you my home and get you something dry to wear."

"Then can I explore?" she asked. She felt like a kid on Christmas morning.

He helped her to her feet, and she clung to his hand as they walked across the beach and onto a path. She could hear voices ahead and nerves started to build. "Is everyone here a vampire?"

"Mostly, yes. There are a few sea witches, and some mermaids pass through from time to time. The prison, of course, holds beasts of all kinds."

"Mermaids," she whispered in awe of this world she'd stumbled into.

"Yeah, not as sweet as humans like to think. Mermaids are... sly. Never enter into a deal with one."

"Noted," she said with a giggle. It all seemed so unreal. Mermaids and sea witches, vampires, werewolves, and monsters! "Oh my, I'm not in Kansas anymore."

"You were in Miami, Katherine. Are you sure you're alright?" he asked with concern, stopping, and turning her to look at him. His eyes bore into hers as if he were searching for a sign of brain damage.

She just laughed. "Yes, I'm fine. It's just a saying, a human saying."

They continued down the path and she tried to ignore the prickles of nerves. This was a world she knew almost nothing about.

"Ian! You returned," came a booming voice as the path opened before a huge stone wall. There was no gate, but there was a huge archway and under it stood a giant of a man in a leather kilt and two swords strapped to a belt. He had long black hair that was braided to his waist, and his smile was wide and welcoming.

"Thorn! It's good to see you at the gate. Has all been well?"

"All has been splendid, my Prince," he said, his eyes landing on Katherine. "I see you have not arrived alone."

"This is Katherine. She is a Descendant, and she is my mate," he declared simply.

Katherine nearly choked on that statement but didn't think now was a good time to discuss the status of their relationship.

Thorn's eyes went wide, and he fell to a knee, his head bowed, and his body seemed to tremble. "A Descendant, my gods, Ian. Will she be safe here?"

That was an unexpected statement. Katherine pulled back and looked at Ian with wide eyes and open mouth. "Safe?" she hissed, shaking her head slightly.

"Get up, you ass. Of course she will be safe. I am in charge, and she is mine." His words were gruff and less than reassuring.

Thorn stood, but he stepped back, away from her and looked unsure. "I will alert the others. We will go hunting this night in larger shifts to make sure everyone is sated. Will there be a celebration at daybreak?"

"Yes, and then I must call a meeting with you and Saul."

Thorn nodded and turned as if he were in a great hurry to get away.

Ian turned to her and had the decency to look embarrassed. "Your blood will be quite tempting to the others, but I assure you, you are safe. I have claimed you; they wouldn't dare harm you; you belong to me."

Katherine rubbed a hand over her face and groaned. "I don't want to have to *belong* to you to be safe, Ian. Maybe I should have stayed in Miami." She held onto anger at his deception. It kept the fear back.

"No one here would harm you no matter what. It's not what we do. I just mean that because you are mine, they will not even try to seduce you into giving them a sip," he said with a wink and a devilish smile. "Come, love, you need dry clothes."

She wanted to argue but had no real option but to go with him. It wasn't as if she could get home on her own.

They walked through the archway and onto cobblestone streets. It looked like a village taken straight out of a history book, if that history book had somehow mashed together both Greek and Egyptian architecture. Little homes and shops were scattered around the large pyramid she'd seen sticking out from the beach and the Parthenon structure held a large garden it looked like. She really hoped they'd get to visit there. What treasures would she find here, perfectly preserved and unseen by humans for so long? Men stood here and there, calling out a greeting to Ian, but none came close for conversation, and none acknowledged her, but their eyes swept over her with curiosity and something more. Her anxiety built as they moved deeper into the village, right to the base of the pyramid.

Ian stopped before a large door set into the stone base.

"You live in a fucking pyramid?" she gasped; her anxiety momentarily forgotten.

"Part of it, yes. Parts are used as public meeting places and, of course, the basement holds the prison."

"That's pretty awesome."

"I'm glad you approve."

"I live in a one-bedroom apartment," she frowned. "You probably thought it was terrible," she said with an uncomfortable laugh.

"I thought it was perfectly charming, and the bed was particularly delightful," he said with a low growl. He pulled her into his arms and kissed her firmly. "Now let me show you mine."

He led her inside a dimly lit hallway and up so many stairs she thought for sure they were about to reach the peak. When he stopped finally and opened a door, she would have been happy with anything. She was shocked to find herself standing in a bedroom with a huge bed, thick wood posts, a soft red cover, and so many pillows she thought she could make a whole other bed just with them. There was a small green fainting couch, a desk of dark wood with a matching chair. There were rich colored rugs and artwork that looked slightly water damaged, but still impressive. "Did—did you get this stuff from shipwrecks?" she asked, realizing what she was seeing couldn't have been here when Atlantis sank.

"It didn't make sense to leave behind the goods when we took the blood," he said simply. "When we were into that sort of thing."

"Right," she agreed, a little uncomfortable.

Her nerves were quickly pushed aside as he grabbed her wet dress and pulled it over her head, then frowned at her swimsuit and peeled it off her body. "You'll need proper clothing."

"No one seemed to be very thoroughly dressed," she pointed out. In fact, she was certain no one had been wearing more than a kilt in the entire village.

"Clothing gets in the way when fighting," he said with a shrug. "In fact, we have all seen each other naked many times. It is how we usually swim and hunt."

"Oh," she said, face reddening as images floated into her head of Ian and the other very attractive men she'd seen as they walked through the village swimming naked together, hunting whales and dolphins.

She was distracted from thinking of other men when he captured her mouth in a deep kiss and hoisted her into his arms. She wrapped her legs around his waist, and he walked them to the large bed. He laid her down onto the soft mattress and soon she was too busy feeling pleasure to think about anything else that was going on.

Eighteen

IAN LAY with a sleeping and sated Katherine in his arms, staring up at the familiar ceiling of his bedroom. Outside, he could hear the others as they went about their night with a little extra energy. He had known bringing her here was a risky thing, but he would kill to protect her, even from his men. They weren't a real danger. They weren't starved, so they should have no trouble resisting her. Thorn didn't even seem to smell the extra sweetness of her blood until Ian pointed out that she was a Descendant.

He was more worried about her reaction to everything here. He needed her to like it, needed her to accept it. He had no intention of letting her go back above the waterline, ever. Now that he had her, he intended to keep her.

She made a small noise in her sleep, and he held her tighter. A quiet knock at the door had him grumbling and moving silently to answer it.

"What?" he hissed before he saw who it was.

"You're naked," Sparah said with a raised eyebrow. "I guess that means the rumors are true. You brought a mate back from the topside."

Ian smiled broadly at the sea witch. She was one of his dearest friends and he trusted her opinion more than anyone else's in Atlantis. He had no idea how old she was. She'd looked the same since he could remember. Long black hair with a streak of grey at the temple, golden brown skin, bright blue eyes, and a missing ear. That was something she hid with her hair most of the time, but he knew it was there. Something had happened so terrible, even her great power in spell casting hadn't been able to revive the appendage.

"Jealous?" he asked with a sly grin.

"Not in the least. I changed your nappies; I don't want your dick. I do want to meet her though and make sure she's good enough to be queen."

Ian frowned. "I'm not the king."

"You are, even if you refuse to take up the title."

"I never wanted it."

"As if that matters," she said with frustration. They'd had this argument a million times. "Is she really a Descendant?"

"She is, though she didn't know it before I met her."

Sparah looked surprised, something he rarely saw on her face. "Well, where is she?"

"Asleep, but I promise you'll meet her. When she wakes, we'll join the others for a daybreak festivity."

"She'll require human food. I'll bring up a tray and clothing."

"Thank you, Sparah," Ian said and gave the old witch a kiss on the cheek.

He closed the door and walked back to the bed where Katherine slept on soundly. He slipped in beside her and pulled her body close. The skin-to-skin contact was invigorating, and the warmth of her made his fangs descend. Other things were equally affected, but he managed to ignore them all. She needed her rest, she was just a human. His delicate human. The thought brought a smile to his face and scared the crap out of him.

. . .

Katherine woke up with Ian curled around her, his face buried in her neck, breathing in her scent.

"Are you going to bite me?" she asked, half serious. She wasn't sure how she felt about being his regular blood supplier, and she had no idea how often he needed to feed.

"Just enjoying your sweet smell, love."

"How often do you feed?"

"I can go a day or two without blood, no problem."

"But you don't like to," she asked, hearing the reality in his voice.

"No, I prefer to take blood daily." He said simply, pulling away and looking at her with a guarded expression. "You don't have to be my only supplier; you don't have to ever give me blood again if you don't want to. It's not why I brought you here."

Katherine smiled up at him. Those words sounded like truth, and it eased her mind. "I will give you my blood every day, if that's what you need." Especially since the thought of him going to someone else for it made her jealous streak spike like nothing she'd ever experienced before.

Ian's face broke out into a huge grin, and he tucked a lock of her hair behind her ear. "Katherine, you are one amazing woman. How did I get so lucky?"

"My worst day was lucky for you," she said with a laugh.

His face darkened, and she wondered what he was remembering, wondered how horrifying she must have looked after Norgis had left her to die. She shuddered at her own memories of that night.

"I *will* kill him," he said fiercely.

"I know," she whispered. "How soon until we go back to save the others and take care of Norgis and Jovi?"

"Oh! We need to get ready for the celebration," Ian said suddenly, moving out of the bed. "Sparah will be bringing food for you and clothing soon. The sun will rise in an hour."

"Sparah?"

"An old friend."

"Vampire?" Katherine hadn't noticed any females when they'd walked through the little village, but it hadn't struck her as odd until this moment.

"Sea witch."

"Are there *any* female vampires?" Katherine asked

"No."

"Why not?"

"We are warriors," he said simply, as if it were obvious.

"Excuse me, as if a woman couldn't be a warrior?"

"Katherine, females are not warriors," he said placatingly.

She glared at him, ready to defend her internal feminist. "Maybe not in your time, but have you seen female wrestlers? I think they could even kick your ass. Well, if you only had human strength anyway."

"In my time, females were valued far too much to be used as fighters. They were honored as mothers, lovers, and wives. They held great positions of power and importance. They were not subjugated to the ranks of us warriors, bound by our souls to watch over the monsters of earth."

Katherine eased up on her feminist ire a bit at his statement. "Okay, but why haven't any been turned since then. No one wanted to keep a female vampire for eternity?" The realization that if Ian wanted to keep her, she'd grow old and die, but he wouldn't, tried to eke its way into her brain and cause all kinds of anxiety she didn't need. She pushed it back and knew she'd be investigating it thoroughly in the near future.

"It is not an easy thing, to turn a human into a vampire. The risk is great and taking that chance on someone you love is something no warrior has been willing to do."

"Oh," Katherine said softly, looking away from his intent gaze. She was reminded of the werewolves' problem. These monsters were more alike than they would want to admit.

A soft knock at the door halted any further discussion, and she

THE VAMPIRES OF ATLANTIS

was grateful. Her mind was full enough. Ian quickly covered himself with a leather kilt on his way to the door. When he opened it, a beautiful woman walked in. She looked nothing like a witch, except maybe for the long black skirt and the deep green bustier top, which was kind of witchy. She was quite pretty, and a stab of jealousy hit Katherine as she watched the woman touch Ian's arm fondly in greeting and walk into his bedroom as if it were the most normal thing for her to do. This could be the only woman in this place other than her, and Katherine was suddenly sure Ian had slept with her. How could he not, she was gorgeous, full perky breasts and soft red lips. As she walked, her hips swayed gracefully and her smile showed perfect white teeth.

Katherine pulled the bedding up to hide her nakedness and hopefully her ineptness as well.

"Sparah, this is Katherine," Ian said as the woman reached the bed.

"Katherine. What a delight to meet you. Everyone is talking about you, I'm afraid. No secret is safe in Atlantis," she said with a tinkling laugh.

Katherine flushed with embarrassment. She didn't like being the topic of conversation, and the way this woman said it made her feel like it was a shameful thing.

"Of course they are talking of her. Can't you see why?" Ian proclaimed. "She's a sight, and she's all mine. They're jealous."

"Indeed," Sparah agreed and set a tray on the bed. "But does she talk?"

Katherine was sure her face got even redder. "I do, it's nice to meet you, Sparah."

"I brought a few things you might be able to wear since whatever you came in must be soaked."

"That's very thoughtful."

Sparah looked at her with an intensity that Katherine could almost feel for long enough that it was awkward. Katherine didn't know what to do. She was frozen. When the woman straightened with an unreadable expression. Katherine took a breath.

"Well, I'll leave you to it then. See you downstairs."

When the door closed behind Sparah, Katherine raised an eyebrow at Ian. "She's interesting."

Ian laughed. "Will the clothing please you?"

Katherine found a skirt and top, both extremely out of date. "I'm sure it's fine," she said, trying to not worry.

"Good, get dressed. I want to show you around."

He didn't seem to be leaving to give her privacy, so she decided to not act like getting dressed in front of him was more intimate than sex. She pulled on the skirt first, no undergarments in sight. Luckily, she didn't mind going braless, but no panties under a skirt? That felt a little awkward. The skirt was long, hitting her ankles and made of a deep green cotton. It was light enough to flow as she walked, but thick enough that she felt well covered. It came with a wide leather belt that snugged it around her waist. The shirt was a white cotton, obviously a man's she decided as she slipped it over her head. It reached past her ass and the sleeves covered her hands.

"I'm not sure about this," she said as she looked down at herself. The gap between her breasts was fully exposed.

"I think we can make this work," Ian said, going to a drawer and pulling out a needle and thread.

"You sew?" she asked with shock. She couldn't imagine this large man hunched over a garment, making tiny stitches.

"We've all had to learn to do things down here to take care of ourselves."

"Because you didn't have slaves," she said and bit her lip as soon as the words were out.

He gave her a shamed look. "Yeah, because we didn't have our slaves." He sighed heavily. "We didn't treat them poorly," he added. "Most were happy to be a part of what we were doing up there. It was just the idea of being brought down here that got most of them to decide they wanted freedom instead."

"But isn't that because of the Stone? They were only happy with what they were doing because of the Stone?"

Ian nodded. "Maybe so, but we didn't know any different. It had always been that way."

She wasn't sure what to say to that, so she didn't say anything. She stood still while he quickly stitched the front of the shirt to an acceptably modest height. Then she tucked the bottom of it into her skirt and rolled the sleeves. She wasn't going to win best dressed, but this would do.

"Thank you," she said as she stood in front of a mirror, wishing she had a brush and maybe a little mascara.

Ian came up behind her and put his hands on her shoulders. His head and shoulders were visible above and around her; he made her feel tiny, and she loved it. He bent to kiss the top of her head tenderly. "You look lovely. I'll bite anyone who looks at you."

She giggled and turned to embrace him. "Don't bite anyone but me," she said playfully and nipped at his chest.

He made a low growl and pulled her up into his arms, cradling her against his chest, and walked to the bed and dumped her there.

"I thought we needed to go meet everyone," she said, a little breathless.

"They can wait. I need you to do that again."

She watched as he quickly removed his kilt, his eyes dark with passion. When he joined her on the bed, she was thankful for the no undergarments as he slid her skirt up with one hand and grabbed the back of her head with the other.

"I want to wear your mark," he hissed, pulling her head to his chest.

She hesitated, unsure of what exactly he wanted her to do, but when his fingers began to stroke her core, she lost all worry about anything other than feeling and went on instinct. She sank her teeth into his chest, tasting blood. The sound of primal pleasure that came out of his mouth told her she'd done right.

As soon as she pulled her head away, he was covering her with his body, his head at her neck as he entered her, twice.

She screamed her pleasure quickly as the feel of him at her neck spread a fire to meet the one he was stroking between her thighs. He was right behind her, taking his fill in a rapid pulse of strokes, then lifting his head, arching his back, and growling at the ceiling.

It might have been the fastest sexual experience she'd ever had, but it was also the most erotic. Still fully dressed, blood on her mouth, neck, and shirt where his chest had rubbed against her. Skirt pushed up around her waist and him naked and bloody, sweat beading on his chest as he stared down at her like she was the most beautiful, wonderful, precious thing he'd ever seen.

Her heart flipped and her head filled with so much serotonin she thought she might pass out. *Was this what love really felt like?* She wondered.

She reached up and touched the spot of his chest that was already healing, but clearly showed the imprint of her blunt teeth. "I hope that's what you were wanting," she whispered.

"You did perfect, love. I will wear your mark with honor and no other will doubt what we are to each other."

She couldn't help the nerves rising. "What exactly are we?"

"We are mates. We belong to each other. You will give me your blood and I will protect you. We will live in each other's arms, pleasuring each other into eternity," his voice was low and growly at the end, sending a shiver through her.

Then she thought about his words, and it wasn't good. Warning bells started to go off and as the panic started to rise, she was thankful for the loud knock on the door that took his attention away from her before he noticed.

He jumped from the bed, pulling her skirt down as he went and picked up his own to throw over his nakedness as he went to answer it.

She sat up and tried to not look like they'd just gotten done doing what they'd been doing. She ran a hand over her face and it came back a little bloody. "Fuck," she hissed and grabbed the bedding to wipe her face and neck, hopefully clean. Her shirt was a loss though.

Ian had paused with his hand on the door at her word. He looked at her with a shit eating grin and licked his lips. "Vampires always bleed when they have sex. No one is going to think it's odd, dear."

"I'm not a vampire," she grumbled. *Just a dumb human,* she added to herself.

His face showed no concern as he opened the door.

"Ian! I am dying to meet her, bring her out or I swear on your father's grave I am going to bring the army up here to meet her proper."

The threat was said with a mocking tone, but it made Katherine's heart pound and she slipped off the bed and put it between herself and the door, eyes shifting around for a weapon.

"Don't be an ass," another voice called, softer.

Katherine was surprised. It was almost soft enough to be a woman's.

"Did she get some clothing? I brought some things if she needs," the soft voice said again. It wasn't a woman, she decided, but it was certainly, effeminate.

"She has what she needs. We'll be down shortly." Ian glanced over his shoulder and frowned. "Maybe the shirt."

"Great!" came the soft voice and then a tall lanky man forced his way past Ian and waltzed in with a pile of clothes and a huge smile. His red hair was braided in two french braids down his back and he wore slacks rather than the kilts she'd seen on the other men. They were tight and leather and she wondered how he could move so smoothly in them. He was shirtless, and his chest was decorated with an intricate tattoo pattern. "Oh my, she is stunning! I'm Felix and I'm here to make sure you have everything you need. These men are not typically very prepared to care for a woman. Ian hasn't had a woman in a millennium," he laughed.

Ian snorted and Katherine looked at him with wide eyes as Felix continued to chatter about style and how no one around here had any. Beside Ian stood a man as big as him, younger she thought, and grinning from ear to ear, fangs showing.

"Are you going to introduce me?" He asked Ian, jabbing him with an elbow.

"Katherine, this is Saul. You met Felix."

"Hi," she said quietly.

"Oh my, he bit you good, let's clean that," Felix said as he got close. "Ian never did like to share; he wants to make sure you look taken." He laughed. "Like a vampire wedding ring, only more permanent," he laughed.

Every word Felix spoke amped up her anxiety until she thought she was going to scream. She met Ian's eyes across the room as Felix started to pull her tunic up.

"Out," Ian hissed. "Can't you see you're scaring her with your inane chatter?"

Felix froze, her shirt about to expose her breasts. "Scaring her?" he said with surprise. "Oh," he said with disappointment and a little bit of hurt passed over his features before he dropped her shirt and turned. "Well, I guess I'll just wait downstairs like everyone else." He paused at Ian and looked back at her. "It's nice to meet you, Katherine, I think you picked well with Ian here."

Katherine felt like crap. She'd offended him and all he'd been doing was trying to help. "Felix," she said quickly before he could get all the way out of the room. He turned quickly, hope in his eyes. "Maybe you can help with my hair?"

He squealed and rushed over. Her shirt was over her head before she could think of what was happening and he'd pulled another over her head. Luckily Ian had pushed Saul out the door and closed it so no one else got a free peep show. The new shirt was a soft black cotton with a collar and buttons. It was still a little long, but when Felix pulled off her belt and put it over the shirt, she felt like it was all perfect.

He then pushed her into the desk chair and began to braid her hair. Ian slipped out, *to check on things*, he said. She had no idea what that meant, but she didn't care. She felt safe with Felix, and her eyes wandered as he braided. There were so many things in the room it would take a week just to assess it all. So much she could immediately tell belonged in a museum.

"Hold this, love," Felix said and handed her a small silver comb.

She inspected it as he continued his braiding work. It was a beautiful silver comb inlaid with rubies in a geometric pattern. She turned it over in her hand. "The magic of Atlantis keeps these things from aging?" she asked.

"Oh yes, everything is kind of frozen here. You too," he added with a laugh. "Honestly, it's nice to not have to worry about wrinkles and grey hair. All done!"

"Thank you, Felix. I really appreciate the help." She inspected her hair as he pushed the silver comb into place in the back. He'd braided it in two french braids and twisted them in the back to make a fancy sort of style that was very out of date, but she thought it fit here perfectly among all these incalculably valuable artifacts from another time.

"Of course. I am so excited you're here. It will be so fun to have someone to talk to that cares about more than working out and training for battles we'll never fight." He rolled his eyes. "We'll be besties, I'm sure."

"Well, while I'm here. I'll be back up top as soon as Ian figures out what he needs to help the others." She liked the idea of spending time here, wanted to search every building, wanted to catalogue each item. She knew she could spend countless hours enthralled by figuring out where it came from, where it was going when the ship was sunk, or taken down by vampires? She wanted to explore them all. Not to mention what was here when the city sank. It was a treasure trove of, well, treasure!

Felix frowned at her. "Ian is letting you go back up?"

"Letting me!" she snapped. "He can't stop me."

Felix cocked a hip and gave her a pitying look. "Oh honey, you're his female. You think he's going to let you go? Atlantis is the only place you'll be able to live forever without becoming like us, which I know he isn't going to try and do. You have to stay and he's not going to let you leave. But don't worry, it's actually pretty great here."

The panic was back.

Nineteen

IAN SAT with Saul and Thorn, his two most trusted men. "We need a good plan before we go up, and I think I have one."

"You're sure it's necessary? Beltar and Samson surely won't be held in a cage for long."

"It's a cage built with them in mind. You have to remember things have changed up there. The Descendants gained powerful friends, witches, and have enchanted the cell beyond our powers."

"And Jovi?"

Ian wrinkled his brow and clenched his fists. "Jovi will be punished for what he's done. He has taken his desire too far. There is no way we can go back to enslaving the Descendants."

"Because you love one?" Thorn asked with no inflection, as if he didn't care much about the answer.

"Because it's wrong," Ian said firmly. "My father knew it, I know it, and you all know it. Jovi is the only one who doesn't agree."

Thorn looked satisfied with that answer.

"What is your plan?" Saul pressed; his usual joviality subdued with the thoughts of battle.

"I am going to take bigger backup."

"Bigger?" Thorn asked carefully.

"Bigger and older," Ian said with a nod.

"We'll go back with you," Saul said firmly, and Thorn nodded agreement.

Ian smiled at his men. "I was hoping you'd say that. Now, let's go celebrate. We leave at sundown."

He hurried back to his bedroom where he'd left Katherine in the capable hands of Felix. He was surprised to open the door and find her curled in a ball on the bed breathing hard and Felix having a near panic attack as he paced back and forth.

"God almighty! Ian, she—she just flipped, and fell, and screamed, and now this!"

"What the hell did you do?" he roared and rushed to her side, hissing in Felix's direction.

Felix's eyes began to fill with tears and Ian almost felt bad for yelling at the man.

"Nothing, I swear, oh Gods, is she alright? I don't know anything about humans, did I—did I harm her?"

Ian just grunted as he put his face near Katherine's. "My love, what happened?"

"You fucking liar," she whispered. "You are going to lock me up. Lock me away and keep me alive to feed off of me. You are no better than Jovi."

The quiet words sliced through him with such pain, he fell back unable to speak. He couldn't. She was right. "Fucking Gods," he hissed.

"Oh shit," Felix said and hurried out of the room.

Katherine sat up, her eyes red from crying, and it clawed at his heart to know it was his fault.

"It's true. You can't even deny it. Ian, do you really think this is what I want? To live tucked away here and provide for you like a fucking dinner plate? *Really?*"

"I—I just want to keep you safe."

"Safe is one thing, but taking my choices away is another. I won't let you do that," she whispered it but the vehemence in her tone was undeniable. "What if I don't want to live forever," she added, and it was like a stake to his heart.

"No," he hissed and stood.

"No?"

"No, you will stay." He got up and left before she could say anything more, or he could dig the hole he was in any deeper. He was pissed, he was scared, and he wanted to kill something.

"Saul! Thorn!" he called as he headed down the hall. Saul appeared first, but Thorn was only steps behind. "We go now."

"But the sun is nearly up."

He would take them to the caves where Jovi and Norgis had been hiding. They could get there directly from the sea and stay mostly unexposed to the sunlight. He had to get away before he let Katherine's tears change his mind. He couldn't lose her. No matter what.

Ian cursed. "That's fine. I have a plan. Meet me at the beach. I'll grab Vane." Ian hurried down below the pyramid to the prisons beneath.

In the prison there were beasts of all sizes and shapes. Every horror that once walked the earth was tucked away safely here and they all hated him. That was fine with him. He didn't need their cooperation. The magic that held them was stronger than anything that was possible anymore. Born from the belly of a goddess as she sacrificed herself to imprison them, her bones became the bars, and her lover sacrificed himself to protect them all, giving his soul to become the bubble that protected the city at the bottom of the sea. As Ian walked into the prison, he paused by the door where the image of two lovers embracing in the crashing waves of a world of yesterday was carved. He touched them where their fingers twined each other's and gave thanks for the gifts they had given the world. He would not let Jovi or anyone else make their sacrifices worthless.

Ian opened the door and went to the first cell. Staring in at a deadly beast that looked as innocent as a small boy.

"Ian, I expected to see Jovi."

"Why didn't you tell me it was Jovi who came for Norgis."

"I'm no tattletale, despite my boyish good looks," he said with a laugh far too deep to come from a being who looked twelve.

"I need you to help me get him back, and I need you to return to this cell when it's done."

Vane looked at his nails. They were claws really, black and sharp, a clue about how dangerous he was despite the cherubic face. "You need me. What do I get in return?"

Ian clenched his jaw; he had come prepared to negotiate as much as he hated that he had to. "What do you want?"

"Oh, just a witch of my own, a little toy to play with now and then."

Ian could just imagine what this thing would do with a witch, and it was horrifying. "No."

He huffed and rolled his eyes, laying back on his cot. He stuck one arm under his head. "I don't think you're in any position to deny me. You need me because Jovi already won up there, didn't he? Found the Stone, took over the Descendants? And your men? They must be dead or imprisoned themselves. How you escaped is a wonder, but perhaps your brother misjudged how strong you are," he shrugged. "Maybe not. Are you willing to do what it takes to bring them down?" His eyes lit up with anticipation and it made Ian's skin crawl. "I hear you got out with a pretty little prize, too." Vane licked his lips, a bright red tongue darting out to cover his lips with black saliva, and his eyes flashed red. "Oh don't look surprised. I can smell her from here and I'm not the only one. It's been ages since we've had a Descendant around, but we haven't forgotten the sweet smell of their blood."

This was a mistake. Ian turned to leave. He'd find another way. "Did she come to you willingly? Or did she put up a fight? I always liked it when they fought back."

Ian turned and hissed, showing Vane his fangs and grabbing the bars of his cell. "Listen carefully, Vane, if you even think of her, I'll rip your head off. Do you understand me?"

Vane only laughed. "If only you could, then we'd all be dead. But you can't, so here we are. Now the only real question is. What are you willing to give me to go along with your little plan and return to this nice little cage that was made special just for me?"

Ian couldn't kill them, it was true. All these monsters were immortal, which is why they'd had to accept the same curse to keep them in their cages. It didn't mean he couldn't harm and hurt them, though, and he really wanted to torture the little shit that was standing smugly before him, but he needed his help. "I'll give you one night of freedom above."

"Oh!" Vane's eyes lit up and Ian's gut wrenched. Vane could do a lot of damage in one night, but Norgis and Jovi would do a lot more if they were allowed to continue unimpeded.

"One sundown-to-sunup and then you're back here. We'll write a contract in blood and if you try to skip out, I'll call on it to burn you where you sit."

Vane looked thoughtful but Ian knew he'd take the deal. It was more than any of these monsters had been given a chance at in thousands of years.

"You've got yourself a deal, Ian," he said with a sickening smile.

"I'll send Sparah down with the contract, you'll bleed, then we'll leave."

"Wonderful, and which form will you be desiring for this quest?"

"When it's time, you'll go in as your largest form."

"Oh, how wonderful, a chance to really stretch."

Ian walked away feeling disgusted, but he had no choice. This was the guarantee he needed to stop Jovi and save his men. He wished the feeling didn't mirror what he was currently feeling about keeping Katherine here to keep her safe and with him.

He pushed those thoughts aside as he went to Sparah's room

to have her write up the contract. He wasn't surprised to see her at her desk with pen in hand. "I assume you're putting a contract in place before taking that monster up."

"You know me well, Sparah."

She smiled at him fondly. "I do, which is also why I must advise you *not* to follow your instincts where the girl is concerned. She has a mind of her own. She will not be kept. You'll destroy any chance with her if you try and keep her here against her will."

Ian clenched his jaw. "Just write up the contract for Vane," he snapped. "He gets one night above, sundown-to-sunup. After we contain Norgis and Jovi, obtain the Descendant's Stone, and release my men from the prison below their compound."

Sparah pursed her lips and looked thoughtful. "I'll write it up, give me your blood." Ian held out his hand, and she took a shining crystal knife out of a drawer, she pierced his palm, and he turned his hand, letting it drip onto the parchment she would invoke with a spell to bind the contract.

As she mumbled and her spoken words appeared on the page Ian had a sudden panic. His blood wasn't solely his own! He'd recently drank from Katherine and her from him; would that impact the agreement?

"We shared blood today," he said as the witch finished working her spell. "Will that matter?"

"Not as long as she stays close, the spell ensures that Vane can't get more than a thousand feet from you or her," she said with a shrug.

Anger flowed through him. "You knew this was going to happen," he accused.

"Yes, and I also know that if you try and keep her here, she is going to die trying to escape." Sparah looked at him with such a serious look he froze. "I like her. She's strong, and that's exactly what you need. Don't fuck it up."

He knew Sparah sometimes saw the future, and it was never

wrong. She'd foreseen his father's death and been unable to stop it, no matter that she'd loved him. "I can't lose her," he whispered.

"If you try, and make her stay, if she becomes your prisoner, you have lost her."

"I won't lose her," he said more firmly. "Take that to Vane and get his blood."

Ian left Sparah's chambers and hurried back to his own. He threw open the door and let loose a vicious growl. It was empty.

Katherine was running, and she didn't know where she was going or what she was going to do, but there was no way in hell she was about to spend the rest of her life cooped up in a fucking pyramid on a sunken island city under the ocean. She may be dead for all anyone knew, but she still had a life. She could still reclaim her apartment and job and live a normal, well sort of normal, life. This was insane, no matter how blood-boiling and toe-curling the sex was. She was not being held prisoner with a bunch of bloodthirsty men in kilts.

"Woman!" A loud voice roared as she got to the archway she'd entered the city through.

She didn't stop, her bare feet pounded faster, and her legs burned with the effort, but she sped up, and head down, barreled ahead.

"Stop!" the voice shouted again and this time she heard running feet.

"Shit," she gasped, but she didn't dare look.

"What's all this?" A loud voice asked as she hit the path through the jungle.

"That's Ian's mate, she's trying to get away!"

"Why?" came the confused reply. He wasn't chasing her, but the other's voice was getting closer fast.

"Fucked if I know," the first voice said as his hand landed on her shoulder, stopping her abruptly. She fell back against a large chest and then, most horrifyingly, she cried. She crumpled to the ground at his feet in a heap and she cried.

"I don't want to be his blood bag prisoner," she whimpered.

"Um, you made her cry, you idiot," said the second voice.

"Shut up and go find Ian." The man crouched down but didn't touch her.

After a moment, the tears mostly stopped, and she looked up. She recognized him. This was the one who had been at the gate earlier, Thorn. He had a friendly face. Maybe he would take her back. "Will you help me? I need to get back. I can't stay here," she pleaded.

Thorn's face looked pained. "I would never wish you harm, love, but if I helped you escape, Ian would turn me inside out and feed me to the monsters."

"I'm going to die here," she whispered.

"Have you talked to him?"

She rolled her eyes. "He said no and stormed out. I've been in toxic relationships before. I know the warning signs." That wasn't exactly true, but she'd watched enough shows to recognize it.

"Toxic huh, well I think perhaps Ian has forgotten how to treat a woman."

"But you won't help me?" she whined and hated that she was acting like a weak ass female. This was not how the romance novel heroine was supposed to act.

"I'm sorry, not the way you want, no." Thorn stood and tears spilled out of her eyes again.

Then a guttural hiss brought her attention up in time to see Thorn go flying into a nearby tree. "Why does my mate weep at your feet!"

Ian stood there, his eyes glowing in rage and his chest heaving, his hands were fisted, and he looked ready to kill. Katherine should have been frightened. She should have skittered away, screamed perhaps, but instead she stood up and did something that was probably considered insane.

She slapped him.

No sound was heard anywhere. It was like the entire island was holding its breath to see what Ian would do. He stared at her, eyes wide, mouth open in shock.

"How dare you," she seethed. "How dare you assume you can make decisions for me. How dare you think you can keep me against my will, and how dare you push your friend." She had her hands on her hips and welcomed the anger replacing the despair she'd been feeling moments before.

"Me? How dare he! What did he do to you?"

"Only tried to stop me from escaping *you*," she said, poking her finger into his chest for emphasis. "Only *listened* to what I had to say instead of storming off," she snapped.

"Oh, she's defending you, Thorn, you should probably run and hide. Ian is going to kill you," the other vampire was back and laughing at his friend.

"Katherine," Ian said in a breath and put his hands on her cheeks. His whole body softened as he stared into her eyes. "I wish to only keep you safe and with me. Is that so terrible?"

"Yes, yes, it is when you gave me no choice, no information or option. Ian, I don't know that this is what I want as my forever. I just don't know."

Sadness filled his eyes and she immediately wanted to take it back, to tell him she would stay, she'd be his everything if he would just never look at her like that again, as if she'd just destroyed his entire universe for fun. "You will return with us," he said quietly.

"Thank you," she whispered.

"Saul is bringing our weapon, a great beast. Vane is dangerous, and I don't want you to get close to him." His gaze was serious as he said this.

"As soon as we are above water, I'll go to my apartment. I'll be safe."

"No."

"No?" she said with gritted teeth. He was telling her no, again?

"No, you must stay within a thousand feet of me and Vane."

"Excuse me?" she said with a head shake. She wasn't sure she could quite pull off.

"It is a binding contract. Your blood was in my blood and my blood is in you. It was mixed into the parchment he has signed. The agreement is held by magic stronger than me; it will not be broken."

"Are you fucking kidding me?" She threw her arms up in the air and heard both vampires, who were still observing their fight, suck in a breath. This was probably the most entertaining thing they'd seen in a millennium. She felt like she should offer them some damn popcorn. "You weren't being nice? You don't see the error of your ways. You *have* to take me up because of a fucking blood contract!" She slapped him again, and she was pretty sure one of the vamps laughed but covered it quickly with a cough.

This time Ian did react. He grabbed her and forced her to him, wrapped his arms around her as if they were iron bars and forced her face inches from his own. "You are mine; I will have you and keep you. You will be safe."

"Fuck you," she spat and as she tried to knee his groin, he moved a leg to block her.

"You will control yourself, little one. You are going to hurt your hands on my muscled body and I can't allow that."

She let out a frustrated sigh but stilled her body. He was right, dammit. She wasn't hurting him. He was a big lump of muscle and her hand did sting.

Twenty

KATHERINE WAS SITTING on the beach next to Thorn hours later. She was back in her swimsuit and sundress and they were waiting for Ian to return with Saul and Vane. The sun was just setting up above and she was yawning even though she'd managed a quick nap during the day, Ian having canceled the planned party when she said she'd rather die than spend time around his blood-sucking idiot friends. She knew she'd made a mistake trying to escape. She'd have been completely screwed once she got this far and walking back with tail tucked between her legs would have been worse than the fight that Thorn had witnessed on the jungle path. That didn't mean she was ready to face his entire army and pretend she was his happy mate, though.

"I'm glad you hit him," Thorn finally said.

She was surprised by this statement. "Why's that?"

"It shows that you aren't a pushover. He could easily dominate a weaker woman, and his instincts to have and keep you are strong. If you weren't a strong person, he'd destroy you with all of that love and desire. He has never had someone like you, someone that he wanted to keep, and he doesn't know how to handle it. He watched his father lose his mother and then the Descendant he loved betrayed him, and he can remember the desperation that almost killed the strongest man he knew. Ian doesn't think he's that strong, never thought he deserved the position he has, but he takes it seriously and hopes to make his father proud. But that insecurity also makes him think he's not strong enough to keep you safe. If his father couldn't do it, how could he?"

Katherine thought on that as they waited. She didn't like that it made her heart ache for Ian. She wanted to wrap him in her arms, kiss his face, and tell him it was all going to be alright. She didn't want to leave him. She just wanted to know she was free to live what kind of life she decided to have when this was all over.

When Ian and Saul appeared on the beach, Katherine was shocked to see the preteen between them, a boy looking no more than twelve and all innocence on his round face.

"Where's Vane?" she wondered aloud, thinking something must have changed.

"Wow, Ian, you didn't tell me your mate was more beautiful than Aphrodite. I think I just came in my pants," the preteen looking man said with a voice far too deep for his face.

"Watch your mouth," Ian hissed and put a hand around the boy's throat.

Thorn put a protective arm in front of Katherine and the boy laughed. Ian pulled his hand away with a grunt of pain, and the smell of burning flesh surrounded them.

"No touching," Vane said with a wink at Katherine. "Unless it's her, she can touch me any time."

Katherine couldn't help a shiver and she stepped further behind Thorn.

"Why him, again?" Saul asked with a grunt.

"Because he can get the damn job done," Ian said, looking down at his hand with a frown.

Katherine pushed Thorn's arm aside and went to Ian, careful to stay far from Vane. "Let me see." She took his hand and was glad to see it almost completely healed already.

"I'm fine," he whispered.

She looked up at him and saw a tinge of relief in his eyes and she almost felt bad about her freakout before dawn, but then again, she was still pretty sure he deserved it. She might have decided to forgive him, but she was definitely not ready to tell him that.

"Are you ready?" he asked gently.

"I'm ready."

"Let's do this!" Vane said, rubbing his hands together.

Katherine shuddered as she noticed his black clawed nails. This was no boy at all. What was going to keep him from destroying everyone in Miami?

"I will take Katherine. You two flank Vane and stay behind. The sun is down, but there will be many humans around, so when we surface, keep him between you. He doesn't leave our sight until after the deed is done."

"Then you're letting him loose?" Katherine asked in shock.

"He bargained for a night, he'll get it, it's less damage than Norgis and Jovi plan to do if they aren't stopped." Ian sounded pained, and that was enough to tell her that he was doing what he thought was best and would make for the fewest casualties.

Katherine wasn't sure how she felt about that, but she was in no position to argue, apparently blood bound to that very agreement.

She stepped into the water with Ian, and as mad as she was, she trusted him completely. When he told her to swim, to take a breath and then go down, she did it without hesitation. Just as when they'd arrived in Atlantis, she didn't think she'd make it by the end, sucked through a whirl of water, kicking furiously to reach the top when it stopped and bursting out into the fresh Miami sea air. She wanted to cry. She was so relieved to be out of Atlantis. She didn't wait for Ian to tell her what to do. She started swimming toward shore. She heard the others burst out behind her, but she kept going and when she got tired, she flipped over onto her back and floated.

Ian swam beside her, his breathing not even labored. "I'm going to pull you in."

"Okay," she said with a sigh.

Ian dragged her the rest of the way to the beach with seemingly little effort. The others made the trip underwater, not needing to breathe, apparently, and as their group rose onto the sand, there was more than one gasp from a nearby beach straggler.

"Fuck me," Saul said and when Katherine looked at him, she could see he was leering at some women in bikinis who were stupidly smiling back as if they didn't have any sense for their own safety.

Katherine elbowed Ian and gave him a pointed look.

"We are on a mission," Ian hissed, and Saul winked at the women before standing straight and giving Ian a nod.

"Oh, I can't wait for my reward," Vane said with a giddiness that made Katherine's stomach turn.

"Follow," he instructed and started walking across the sand. Expecting that no one would dare disobey, apparently. He froze when they got to the path and looked at Katherine with a sheepish grin. "Do you have transportation?"

Katherine pursed her lips and crossed her arms. "Yes, I have a car, unless me being dead has given someone else the right to it in the last week."

"We'll need to make it light tight. I'll drive through the night, and you can drive in daylight. We can waste no time," Ian explained.

"It'll never work," she assured him. "I drive a little sports car, cute for me, not for me and three hulking monsters and one small monster."

"I'm not small where it counts," Vane said happily.

"Then we take one," Ian said without a care and started walking again.

"Take one?"

"We have no time to lose, Katherine. We travel by car, and we don't wait for the sun to be down to finish the trip. I will not have the Descendants under Jovi's control any longer than necessary," he said firmly.

That got her attention. Suddenly, she was imagining all the nasty things Jovi could be doing to them without their ability to say no. She shuddered; thankful she wasn't in that position.

It took about an hour, but they found a windowless van and Thorn *convinced* the owner to give them the keys. Then they were on their way out of the city. Ian drove with Katherine giving instructions from the passenger seat on how, and was terrified that they were not going to make it out of the city alive, but he caught on quickly. Thorn and Saul were in the back with Vane where they would remain, safe from the sun. Ian would have to join them back there at sunrise and Katherine would continue the trip. She wasn't excited about that, but she knew she couldn't say he wasn't right. They had to help the others as quickly as possible. A couple hours after sundown the next night, they were parked in front of the compound. The wards were still down, and it was easy to see the impressive wall and building behind. It was eerily quiet, and Katherine had a bad feeling about that.

"Now what?" she asked as they all stared at the closed gate. The house beyond had lights on, but there was no visible movement anywhere. The stench of Norgis was on the air and something else she couldn't identify.

"I smell blood," Vane said with delight. "Jovi is bleeding his livestock."

Katherine stiffened at Vane's words.

"No time to waste," Ian said, giving Vane a nod.

"I'd tell you to look away, but if you're fucking him, I guess you're into monsters," Vane said and gave her a wink.

His body grew and grew, soon he was standing eight feet tall with pure black skin, glowing red eyes, and hair the color of flames.

His teeth shone brilliantly white in his mouth, large and sharp, his claws even more pronounced, and as much as she tried to ignore it, nude. He preened a bit when he saw her glance at what was now about head height to her and she stepped away, allowing Ian to step in between them with a hiss.

"Oh, come now, Ian, jealous?" he said in a voice that was now as deep as you'd expect from a creature so large.

"Get on with it," Ian said, motioning to the gate.

One swift kick had the gate blown open and their group walked in unhindered. No shouts of alarm went up, no sign that anyone was anywhere except for Vane's remark about smelling blood. It was eerie. When they reached the door of the compound, they got their first indication of life. It swung open and there stood a nude and glassy eyed Julie with blood smeared on her neck and a lopsided grin on her face.

"Welcome to our home. Please follow me," she said without inflection.

"A puppet," Thorn said with disgust.

Ian grunted agreement and grabbed Katherine's arm. She was thankful for the blood she'd taken from Ian. If it prevented her becoming that, she'd drink from him every day.

Sensing her need for him, Ian stroked her back and gave her a half smile. It didn't ease her mind and dammit, she hated to owe him or want him more than she already did. But she would never let herself become that.

Julie led them through a silent house and into the backyard. The sight that met them was something none could have predicted, and by the stiffening and hissing that came from the vampires she walked with, she knew they were as disturbed as her. All of the Descendants were there, naked and bloody, standing on top of the tall wall that surrounded the compound. A fall from that height would injure perhaps, but not kill under normal circumstances, but these weren't normal circumstances. Below them spears had been set up, each Descendant was poised to fall onto a sharp spear, ending their life instantly, if they were lucky. They waited for the command with smiling faces.

"Jovi, you're insane," Ian hissed.

"I need only two. They can breed me more." He pointed to Julie and Chase stepped forward. He had apparently been setting up the spears for the others.

Norgis was there as well, watching Vane with narrowed eyes. Two monsters from the same prison, how could they not want to work together to stay out? Katherine had a panic welling up inside her as she imagined the worst happening all around.

"I won't let you do this," Ian said.

"You brought Vane to take out Norgis," Jovi said with little care apparent. "But how will you stop me before I give the command? What will your little pet there think of all these people dying in front of you? You helpless to save even one?"

She felt Ian stiffen beside her. She wanted to yell, to tell Ian to save them all, to stop this, but she couldn't, he couldn't. Oh god, this was going to be the end of so many.

"You can have the throne," Ian said, and his words were met with a sharp intake of breath from the other vampires.

Jovi's eyes widened just enough to indicate his surprise at Ian's offer. "I don't want to be bound to Atlantis, brother, I've had a taste of freedom, I want to keep it and I plan to have an easy meal and a willing body or two as well. You can keep that underwater coffin," he scoffed. "Good luck keeping your blood slave there willingly." He looked at Katherine with a sneer and she hated that she cowered from it. "There's a reason why we didn't give the Descendants our blood. A good slave doesn't have its own thoughts."

Katherine couldn't stop herself from reaching out a hand and touching Ian's back for reassurance. "I love him," she shouted, suddenly struck with an idea. "Something you'll never be able to get from anyone, you piece of shit." Her voice trembled slightly, but she was proud of herself, especially when she saw the anger in Jovi's eyes. She'd hit it perfectly. "Your father must have been a very smart man to have picked Ian instead of his older brother. You don't deserve to rule, no one would follow you willingly."

"What the hell are you doing?" Thorn hissed beside her.

"She's baiting the beast," Vane whispered with a laugh. "Smart woman. Maybe I won't eat her."

"Fuck you," Katherine snapped at Vane even as Ian hissed a warning.

"It won't take long for Ian's blood to leave your system and then you'll be just as susceptible to this as any of the others, you bitch," Jovi said, pulling the stone from his pocket and holding it high.

It was what Katherine was hoping for. They had to get it away from Jovi before they could do anything else, or they were going to lose a lot of people.

"I'll have you kneeling in front of me with doe eyes for those remarks," Jovi continued. "Maybe I'll even keep your mind present just enough to know what you're doing so willingly with that pretty mouth of yours."

Ian growled, a possessive, fierce sound that made Katherine's heart flutter a bit. Then he leapt. He was flying through the air, arms stretched out ready to attack Jovi. Jovi couldn't think fast enough. He leapt to meet Ian and Vane took off at a fast clip to smash into Norgis at the same time. The bodies of the two brothers hit with a thud so loud it made Katherine's teeth clatter. Thorn and Saul flanked her as the fight began but as soon as Ian knocked the stone from Jovi's hand Thorn was gone. Lightning quick, he had the stone in his hand and looked like he had no idea what to do with it. He looked at her with a frightened gaze, as if the stone were poison he'd rather not touch.

"Take it to the basement and let the others out. Sorcha will know what to do." She hoped.

Thorn disappeared back into the house and the battle before them raged on. Jovi and Ian were well matched, but Vane was far stronger and smarter than Norgis. He subdued the beast in moments and stood watching the others with a hand around the monster's throat.

Katherine sucked in a breath as Jovi got a leg under Ian's feet and knocked him to the ground. She wanted to rush forward, as if she could do anything to save him.

"He's stronger," Saul reassured her.

Ian hopped up quickly and managed a twist, pulling Jovi to the ground and landing atop him. Then it was over. Katherine didn't know where he'd been hiding it, but Ian pulled a wooden stake out and shoved it through his brother's chest.

Jovi froze instantly, shock clear on his face. "Brother," he wheezed as his skin began to wrinkle and shrink around his desiccating body.

"You cannot live the life of a monster, brother," Ian whispered as Jovi took one last shuddering breath and his body turned to dust.

Katherine turned away and emptied her stomach onto the grass next to Saul as shouts came from the Descendants on the wall.

Twenty-One

IAN STOOD over his brother's ashes and all he cared about was Katherine. He rushed to her side as she unloaded her stomach. He glared at Saul. "Why didn't you take her from here. She didn't need to see that."

"I didn't know she had a weak stomach," Saul said with a shrug. "She sleeps with vampires."

"One vampire," Ian snapped and pushed his friend away so Katherine could have room to breathe.

"I'm okay," she said weakly, straightening up.

Ian pulled her into his arms. "It's over. The spell broke with Jovi's death and Norgis is contained. It's over," Ian reassured her.

"Except that you promised Vane a night of hell on earth, she whispered," a shudder wracking her body.

Ian stiffened. He'd done what he had to do. All that mattered was that Katherine was safe, that she'd said she loved him, and damn if he wasn't ready to give her the world if she'd only promise to never leave him.

"Ian!" Beltar shouted as he emerged into the yard with the others.

"It's done," Ian said, still holding Katherine close as she shuddered.

Sorcha hurried to help Julie and Chase get the others safely off the wall as they shivered and stuttered and tried to cover their nudity. This would be something hard to get over for all of them, but Ian didn't care. He just wanted to get Katherine away from here before she could decide to stay.

"We must get Norgis back to Atlantis," Ian said as the last Descendant was helped to the ground and took off at a run for the compound.

"I'm taking my night, next sunset-to-sunup is mine and I plan to enjoy it thoroughly in the city," Vane said with a sneer. He'd retained his enlarged form, his hand encircling Norgis' neck easily to contain him. The monster had no fight in him now that Jovi was dead anyway. At least he was smart enough to know when he'd lost.

"We could contain Norgis in the basement, but I don't want Vane anywhere near here, or the rest of you," Julie said with all the confidence of someone who'd just won a battle.

No, *thank you*, no appreciation for what Ian had done, how he'd just killed his own brother in their defense. Ian took a steadying breath so he wouldn't snap at the idiotic woman.

"We will head out. There is no reason for us to remain amongst your people and we wouldn't entrust a monster's keeping to you."

Julie huffed and grabbed Sorcha's arm, pulling her along as she headed inside. Samson watched his woman go without a word. Ian wondered at his silence, but it wasn't his place to intervene. He had his own woman problems.

The ride back to the city was long and silent. Stuffed into the van, three vampires, two monsters and Katherine. Ian had sent Beltar and his men on foot. There was no way they'd have fit in this space too. Not only that, he didn't want them in the city while

Vane had his night. The temptation to try and stop the beast would be great, and if they broke the contract, Vane would be free to not return to Atlantis. That was something Ian couldn't risk.

The sun was close to setting when they reached the city.

Katherine gripped the steering wheel tightly. "Where are we going?" she called into the back.

"I want Norgis back in Atlantis as soon as possible," Ian said firmly. "Is there somewhere near the water we can wait out the sun?"

Katherine thought about that. "I think I know of something," she said and drove on. The thought of waiting out the sun anywhere made her feel twitchy. She wanted clean clothes. She wanted her own clothes, and she wanted a glass of wine. She pulled into the empty parking lot of an old strip mall. It was abandoned, but it was only a block from the ocean, so it should do. And it had a covered loading dock entrance so she could back the van right up close to a door and, she assumed between the vampire strength and the monster strength, they could bust it open and get inside without burning up in the sun.

"Hold on," she huffed as she threw the van into reverse and inched back until she was pretty sure they would have just enough room to partially open the van door. If they got a little sunburn, she couldn't really make herself care. "We're here, get out," she said. She was exhausted, the day had been long and the complaints from everyone stuffed in the back had been grating on her nerves all day. Not to mention she'd been stuck in a vehicle with the monster that had nearly killed her. It was more than anyone should have to deal with. At least the monster was subdued. Apparently without Jovi ordering it to do anything, it was content to follow the directions of the others and sit quietly under threat of death from Vane who had returned to his preteen size.

"You doing okay?" Ian asked as the others beat at the door.

She couldn't speak, she just looked at him with what she hoped portrayed the idiocy of his question.

"I am just glad it's almost over," she said as Thorn cheered at their success, busting into the empty building.

The plan was that they would send Norgis back to Atlantis with Thorn and Saul. Then Ian was going to *keep an eye* on Vane as he ran unhindered through the unsuspecting streets of Miami.

What happened next was the real question. Katherine didn't want to give up the surface. She also didn't want to give up Ian. She wanted to keep her promise to the werewolves, and she wanted to explore the treasures of Atlantis.

He gave her a shy grin. "This will be a great place to wait out the next few hours, plenty of room to spread out. Maybe we can find a space to rest inside," Ian said.

"Oh no, I'm not staying here. I want to go to my apartment, and hide until the city is safe again," she added the last as a whisper, her eyes darting to Vane who was standing inside the backroom of what looked like it must have been a sports outlet judging by the leftover displays.

"Katherine, we must stay within a reasonable distance of Vane. I'm sorry, but you will not be able to stay at your apartment this night. I'm certain we can find something suitable here if we look around. Vane needs clothing as well."

"I found some!" Saul shouted and walked forward, offering a jersey and some shorts. Definitely a sporting goods store.

"Great," she gritted, wondering what would happen if she tried to get farther from Vane than the contract stated. Would she burst into flames, or would he be freed of his obligation to return to Atlantis? Neither was something she wanted to find out, so she slumped and turned to look back out the front of the van.

"What if we go to your apartment? We can wait in the van while you go up and you can get some of your own clothes, if it would please you," Ian offered.

"It would," she agreed.

"Back in the van, Vane," Ian ordered. "I trust you two will be able to handle Norgis from here?" he asked Saul and Thorn, who both agreed easily.

"We'll return him to the prison and look forward to all of you returning at next sunrise," Thorn said with a bright smile.

"I can't wait to see your place," Vane said as he got back in the van.

Katherine just grunted, and as soon as she heard the doors close, she was driving.

Next stop was her apartment.

"I'll be down as soon as it's full dark," Katherine promised as she parked in the familiar lot.

"I don't like this," Ian snarled.

"What is going to happen? It's my apartment building," Katherine said and jumped out before Ian could say anything else. She hurried across the lot and punched in the building code, thankful the lobby was empty because she didn't know how she would handle questions.

She hurried to her apartment, glad she didn't see anyone else. She showered and went into her bedroom. She stared at her bed for a time, remembering the passion she had shared with Ian there. Her heart fluttered. She had fallen in love with him. He was a monster of sorts, but he was more. She could tell he wanted to be more, that he held himself to a high standard. His father must have taught him well. Somehow, those lessons hadn't stuck with Jovi.

But what kind of life could that be for her? She read stacks of romance novels, some even involving vampires, and never had the heroine not ended up happily living with the guy that rocked her world. But that wasn't reality. Katherine's hand touched her neck where she could feel the slightest mark where Ian's fangs had slid into her skin.

"Reality isn't what I had always believed," she whispered to herself. Did that mean she was willing to give up all—all—all what? She was dead, basically. Even when no one thought she was dead, she hadn't had much of a life. One friend, no boyfriend, no pets. Just a job and an addiction to escaping reality in the pages of books where women embraced chaos and found passion and love to last eternities.

Twenty-Two

KATHERINE DRESSED in a short skirt and tank top, strapped on sandals, and then spent a little time smoothing out her long black hair and applying enough makeup to help her blue eyes pop and make her full lips kissable.

She felt good when she stepped into the living room and was surprised to find Ian sitting on the couch.

"Where's Vane?" she asked with worry.

"He is hunting in the building; I couldn't convince him to wait a moment after sunset." He said it with nonchalance, but there was a tightness to his eyes. She knew he didn't like what he'd had to agree to.

"Will he kill them?" she whispered as he moved close to her.

"Some, yes, others will only be drained of their energy. He feeds on energy, not blood. If he wants to be careful, he will leave them unmarked and unharmed aside from a day or two feeling very tired."

She could see on his face that he didn't believe Vane would be using a lot of restraint.

"You look beautiful," he said, touching her cheek carefully.

"Thanks." She hated that she felt joy at his compliment. How could anything make her happy when she knew what Vane could be doing. Did she have a right to be anything but miserable?

Yes, she decided, she did. They both did. She'd survived some serious shit, and it wasn't her fault that Vane was here. It wasn't even really Ian's fault, it was Jovi's fault, and he was deservedly dead. This was all just wrapping up loose ends that Jovi picked out.

Ian sighed heavily and she could tell the weight of the entire situation still sat on his shoulders. "I would never ask you to do anything you didn't want to do."

She reached out and touched his arm. "Except go to the bar with a monster that wants to drain the life out of everyone in sight," she said with a frown, wishing she could be flippant about the reality of this night.

Ian clenched his jaw and dropped his hand from her face. "Except that," he agreed.

"Let's get this over with." She grabbed an old purse and threw a few essentials in it, wondering what had happened to the things she'd had with her at work. Probably confiscated by the police. Could she walk into the police station and get the stuff out of the evidence room? She didn't want to answer the questions they'd have, though, had no answers they would accept. She thought of everything she'd have to go through to come back to life, and it was overwhelming. "Maybe you can convince the police to forget about the whole being murdered and missing persons thing," she said with a tight laugh.

"I could," he agreed.

It was something to consider, she decided. It wouldn't smooth out everything for everyone, but it would take out the legal issues at least. To everyone else, she could just say she'd taken a vacation, had a fling, went a little crazy and took some personal days maybe.

She forced the thoughts away; she couldn't think about that decision right now. But her eyes were drawn to Ian's tense jaw, and she ached to ease at least part of his mind. "Ian I—" she stopped short, unsure if she could do it. It still felt like too much.

Ian looked at her intensely like he wanted to say something, but he just offered her his arm. She took it and they walked out of the apartment. Luckily, they didn't meet up with anyone and when they stepped into the fresh air outside, Vane was leaning against the side of the building looking like the cat that ate the canary.

"What a wonderful night. I do miss seeing the sky," Vane said in greeting. "Where shall we go to enjoy some more of these humans?"

"You feed on energy?" Katherine said, suddenly inspired. "Not blood?"

"Yes, I'm much more sophisticated than a vampire, *much* older."

"Incubus?" she asked.

"Yes, that would be a modern interpretation of it, I suppose." He looked pleased by her curiosity and it creeped her out.

She took a step closer to Ian, grabbing his arm for courage. "What if I could offer you the energy of a hundred writhing bodies, but you must not kill anyone? Could you do that? All at once?"

"Does your female speak of an orgy, because I could be into that," Vane asked Ian.

"I speak of a rave, and I'll only take you if you promise to leave them all alive. You'll get your fill of energy easily there, I don't doubt, but you won't have to take too much from anyone."

"Humans tend to be very attached to the lives of each other," Vane said with a laugh. "Do you know that Norgis is my son and I would have killed him on the spot without a second thought if that had been the deal Ian had made? I can kill him, because I'm a more powerful monster than Ian. Ian can only contain us because that is what the goddess gifted the vampires with, but me. I *am* a god! I feel nothing for anyone beyond myself and it makes you weak, it makes Ian weak, and it makes me the most powerful God that ever walked this earth." He puffed as he spoke, his skin darkening and his eyes gaining a glow.

"Don't break the deal," Ian hissed. "You may have ruled once, but now you're a prisoner of Atlantis like all those other beasts and if you attack either of us, the deal is void and you return without your precious energy."

Vane let out a huff of smoky air and returned to his previous form. "Don't insult me with your care for humans," he warned Katherine. "My deal doesn't prevent the death of them, and I've already killed three in your building."

Katherine was shocked. Her mouth gaped, and she couldn't respond.

"Let's go. You can drink all the energy you need, as Katherine said," Ian prompted, laying a hand to her back.

Katherine was certain she was making a mistake, but she took them downtown anyway. Obviously, she had underestimated Vane. He *wanted* to kill, but this was still the best plan she could come up with. Offering him the energy of a few hundred, surely, he couldn't kill them all, she hoped. They got to the entrance of the underground club and Ian used his vampire influence to make the bouncer let them in without paying or waiting in line.

When they walked in, the music bumped loudly, and she let it wash her mind of some of her worry. Vane made an excited squeal and disappeared into the crowd. Ian guided her to a dark corner where they could observe.

"Do you think he's going to kill them all? *Can* he kill them all?"

"He can," Ian said without hesitation, and her stomach clenched. "But perhaps he will not."

Katherine wasn't eased.

Within minutes, Katherine saw the first one affected. A young woman walked by with a face so pale she looked near death. She collapsed into a chair and her friends flocked to her with concern.

She waved them off weakly but was carried out of the building when it became obvious she wasn't alright. They would assume she'd been drugged, or perhaps just drank too much. Her friends were getting out lucky to leave now unharmed. The urge to scream 'fire' and watch the building empty clawed at Katherine's throat, but she knew it wouldn't do any good. If she pissed Vane off, he'd only kill more.

She saw the same thing again and again. Humans stumbling past looking pale and confused, Vane wasn't killing anyone outright, but Katherine wondered if they'd really recover from the energy drain.

"No!" Ian growled and seconds later a man stumbled in front of them, pale and bleeding.

Ian stiffened beside her and she reached out to him, grasping his arm and offering silent support.

"Play with me," Vane called from somewhere among the crowd.

Another bleeding body stumbled near and dropped to the floor, then chaos erupted in the room. Everyone was screaming and running to get out and as they moved toward the door. It became obvious that the floor was littered with bodies. Some bleeding heavily. Vane was trying to get Ian to kill with him. Trying to trip his bloodlust into a frenzy!

"Oh God," Katherine screamed as the thought filled her mind.

"I don't need their blood," Ian hissed.

"Because of her," Vane scoffed, looking satisfied among his dead.

The screaming and running continued. There would be sirens soon. Police had no doubt been called already. They had to get out of there. "Let's go," Katherine whined.

"Because I'm not a monster. *I'm* not locked up in Atlantis. I protect the earth from the monsters like you," Ian hissed.

"You failed," Vane said, his eyes burning bright red, and wings popped out behind him.

"Your wings were clipped, Vane," Ian said with hesitation.

"But all this power, all this delicious energy your female brought me to, it did much to fix what was stolen from me."

"I—I—" Katherine stuttered.

"No, I can see the tears. You'll never fly again," Ian said with relief.

Vane grabbed a wing and frowned. "Perhaps, but I'm still an impressive sight and they taste so much better when their energy is laced with fear of the devil, don't you think? I can see your blood-lust, Ian. Come, taste this one, it's still alive." Vane pulled up the body of a woman. "We could rule together up here," he whispered.

Ian shuddered as blood dribbled down the woman's neck and thigh.

Katherine had no idea how hard it must be to resist, for Ian to say no to all the fresh blood. His grip on her was painful.

"Ian," she said quietly, reaching up to touch his shoulder. "Ian, I'm here. I'm not going anywhere, and I have everything you need."

"Oh, how sweet," Vane said with disgust. "A filthy human thinks she can be enough for a god! Ian is the vampire king! Whether he accepts the title or not, he doesn't need to bow down to your stupid humanity. He needs to take, to control and slake his bloodlust from anywhere and everywhere!" Vane threw the woman at them.

Ian caught her, dropping Katherine's arm and for a second she thought she'd lost, thought she was going to watch Ian devour this poor woman in front of her. It would be unrecoverable for them, she knew it.

After a tense moment, he turned with stiff movements and set the woman down gently. "Vane, you have but a few hours left. I suggest you spend it more wisely than trying to tempt me away from Katherine and my duty to humans."

Sirens blared in the distance, making them all turn and look at the doors. The building was empty of anyone moving, aside from the three of them.

"We should go," Ian said, grabbing Katherine's arm again, his grip firm but not painful. He was back in control, he'd won the fight against the instincts Vane had tried to engage.

"See you at sunrise," Vane said and moved lighting quick out the door.

Ian pulled Katherine up into his arms and raced toward the door. They emerged into an empty parking lot, but he didn't stop until they were far enough away that they couldn't be easily associated with the horrors that had taken place.

"Do we need to follow him?" she asked with a shaking voice when he set her back on her feet.

"No," he hissed, then put a hand on her back and started moving again. When he stopped below a window she recognized, she was relieved.

"The safehouse?"

"We will wait out the night here. He can do his damage within the space of us."

She hated that they had no other choice; but climbed the stairs thankfully and into the familiar apartment where she'd first woken to him. It was easy to tell when Vane went too far. There was a slight tug and then it eased. He was pushing his limits, but he couldn't go farther than the contract stated and with her and Ian together, apparently, they won the battle of where the circle was centered.

Katherine laid on the couch and stared at the blank television while Ian paced about the room. She was in the middle of a nightmare with the man of her dreams. She glanced at him as he paced. Was she going to embrace the dark so she could have the one who'd swept her off her feet?

Twenty-Three

IAN WANTED TO SCREAM, he wanted to rage, and he wanted to kill Vane. The monster had almost made him flip, had almost tempted him into what he fought so hard against. The only thing that had stopped him was the knowledge that he'd lose Katherine forever. Even if she wasn't going to join him in Atlantis, he couldn't stand living knowing she thought he was a monster. That would kill him.

Now he had to watch her process the horrors that Vane had done, the horrors he was continuing to do out there unchecked. But that was the deal. No other could have so easily subdued Norgis. It takes a bigger monster to take down a monster.

So what did that make him? That question twisted his gut.

When it was time to go, Katherine was finally sleeping, slumped over on the couch. He hated to wake her, but had no choice. She had to go back with them. The contract assured it.

"Katherine, love," he whispered, brushing her hair from her face. She was so beautiful, and his heart squeezed at the softness of her eyes as she looked at him. But when they turned wary and hard, he knew she was remembering what was going on. "We have to go; the sun will rise soon."

She didn't speak, just nodded, and stood with head held high. He guided her out of the apartment and to the street where Vane stood waiting, leaning against the building. He was back in his preteen form. In all the years he'd known Vane, this was his preferred form. It lulled most into thinking he wasn't the most dangerous thing in existence. Even when he'd been worshiped as a god, he'd been in this form most of the time.

"I hope you two had half as much fun as I did," Vane said with a laugh.

Ian just grunted and walked with a guiding arm around Katherine's back. The smell of blood permeated the city air. Vane had done a lot of damage.

When they stood with the water lapping at their feet, she finally spoke. "Can we take a boat out again?" she asked quietly. "I don't think I can swim that far."

"Of course," Ian said softly.

Vane just snorted a laugh as they once again *borrowed* a boat and headed out to the triangle. Vane jumped in as soon as they stopped and began to sink. Ian wasn't worried, there would be guards on alert for his arrival. He'd be taken to the prison immediately and his powers and strength were dulled in the triangle anyway.

"Perhaps you can wait here? The contract might be satisfied as soon as he reaches the vortex," Ian said carefully.

The look on her face was indecipherable, and it made his stomach hurt. He wanted her more than anything, but he couldn't force her, wouldn't. Against every instinct he had, he would let her go.

"You don't want me to come with you?" she said quietly, hurt filling her eyes.

Her words were like a punch to the gut. "I want you more than anything, but, Katherine, I have to be there. I have to finally accept my place as king and I have to make sure nothing like this can happen again. We have become complacent. I can't risk another monster being let out, the earth won't survive, I—"

She held up a delicate hand, and he stopped. She hung her head and her black hair shifted in front of her face to hide her expression. "I understand. You have to go be king."

"No," he said firmly and grabbed her chin, forcing her to meet his eyes. "You don't understand." He pressed his lips to hers and she immediately melted against him. His tongue darted out to slip between her lips, and she moaned as he devoured her mouth with his. When he pulled away, he could feel the sting of sunlight starting to come up over the horizon. He was out of time. "I want you to come be my queen, but I won't force you to live a life you don't want. I won't be one of the monsters I've worked to protect your kind from."

She lifted a hand and touched his face gently. "You are no monster, Ian," she said firmly, then before he could react, she jumped out of the boat. She didn't surface, she was swimming down!

Ian jumped in, quickly moving with sure strokes. He reached her fast and pulled her along to the vortex. He held her close as it sucked them in and pushed them along until they emerged in the warm waters of Atlantis.

"Welcome home," he said and captured her mouth in another deep kiss as soon as they were out of the water. He had her. She would be his forever, and he had a renewed understanding of what his life was being lived for. "My queen," he said as the kiss broke.

A cheer went up, and he turned to see Thorn standing on the beach with Vane.

"I see she chose you," Vane said with a frown. "Stupid human."

"I like her," Thorn said with a smile and tugged Vane toward his prison. "Maybe she has a friend for me," Thorn threw him over his shoulder as they disappeared on the jungle path.

"I don't have any friends," Katherine said with a laugh. "If I'm going to be surrounded by artifacts, I want to catalogue some and take them up for the museum. I can anonymously donate things. No one will have to know it's me."

She was filled with joy over the purpose that would give her, the excitement of discovery, and she would even try and convince Ian to take her traveling. They really could do some amazing discovering with his ability to not have to breathe under water. "I'm also still going to find that Stone for the werewolves." She spoke fast, as if she needed to get it all out before she committed to being here with him.

"You said you would be everything I need," Ian reminded her as he pulled her to the beach. "I will be everything you need as well, my love. I want you forever, however I can have you and if that means spending time above, then we'll work it out. My blood should be enough to stave off aging for short periods of time outside of Atlantis," he said with a grin.

The smile she gave him melted his insides, and he was suddenly in a very big hurry to get her back to his chambers and into his bed.

Please Review

We hope you enjoyed
The Vampires of Atlantis, book one in the Atlantis series, by
Courtney Davis.
If you did, we would ask that you please rate and review this title.
Every review helps our authors.

Rate and Review: The Vampires of Atlantis

Meet The Author

Courtney Davis is an author living in north Idaho with her family and pets. She's a teacher during the day and a writer by night. In her spare time she loves to enjoy her family and the outdoor activities, as long as its warm, that living in the mountains and near a lake offer. Never short on ideas she hopes to fill a library with her own books someday, even if it is a very small library, perhaps one of those little free libraries you see on the street...

Other Titles from 5 Prince Publishing

Liz's Road Trip *Bernadette Marie*
Back to the 80s *S.E. Reichert & Kerrie Flanagan*
Granting Katelyn *S.E. Reichert*
Ghosts of Alda *Russell Archey*
The Serpent and the Firefly *Courtney Davis*
Raising Elle *S.E. Reichert*
Rom Com Movie Club No.3 *Bernadette Marie*
Rom Com Movie Club No.2 *Bernadette Marie*
Rom Com Movie Club No.1 *Bernadette Marie*
A Crossbow Christmas *Ann Swann*
Hot For Teacher *Felicia Carparelli*
The Happily Ever After Bookstore *Bernadette Marie*
Perfect Mrs Claus *Barbara Matteson*
Princess of Prias *Courtney Davis*
Paige and the Reluctant Artist *Darci Garcia*